# Victoria Run

## A Blue in Kamloops Novel

Alex McGilvery

Victoria Run
Alex McGilvery

ISBN 978-1-989092-68-2

While some locations are real, all events and characters are fictional.

# Chapter 1

**Tuesday, September 3**

If Molly hadn't been so nervous, she'd have laughed. She looked at her Community Social Work class at Thompson Rivers University. Her classmates' eyes couldn't be wider if she'd brought a gun and waved it about. They sat in theatre style, maybe thirty of them. She still didn't know most of their names. Even the students she knew were hidden by Covid masks and the dim lighting. She'd been picked to give the first presentation on a group needing social services and the barriers to helping them. She went with what she knew. That might have been a mistake.

"Sex workers can't be lumped into one homogenous group. Some choose the work; others are trafficked against their will. In the middle are those who fall into the life through circumstance. To work with this group, we must first understand the complexity of the life." Molly controlled the huge sigh she wanted to give and smiled.

"Thank you, Molly, you've given all of us something to think about. Assumptions are dangerous. Any questions?" Professor Tatianna Czysiki looked around the room.

"The common perception in the media is that sex workers are addicted to drugs. How prevalent is that?"

"Addiction on the street is whole other topic. Some choose to use drugs for recreation. Some are forced into addiction, then forced to sell themselves to pay for the drugs. I used drugs because it was the only way I could survive." *Shit, maybe they won't pick up on it.*

"What are you doing tonight?" A male voice called from the back. Nervous laughter ran through the room.

The professor's voice cracked like a whip. "Cameron, stand up and apologize."

"It was just a joke." A student slumped to his feet.

"It was sexual harassment." Her voice had no give in it. "Apologise or leave the class."

"I need this class to graduate." He straightened and glared at Molly.

"I'm waiting, Mr. Robinson" Professor Czysiki crossed her arms.

"Sorry." He dropped to his seat with a frown.

"A social worker cannot afford to speak without thinking. Say the wrong thing at the wrong time and you can do incalculable damage to your ability to work with a community." Professor Czysiki nodded at

Molly, who stumbled to her seat. "Scratch many of the best social workers and you will find someone with a broken past who is determined to keep others from being broken the same way." The professor's eyes swept the class like lasers. "That's all our time for today."

Molly gathered her books and looked for the closest exit. Others from the class crowded around her.

"I'd never even imagined…"

"You're so brave…"

A blonde girl broke through the group, wrapped her arms around Molly and sobbed. Molly dropped her books and held the young woman, half fearing she would collapse.

"Maybe leave us alone. I will answer your questions another time." Molly tightened her arms around the weeping girl.

They nodded and almost tiptoed out of the classroom.

After five minutes the sobs began to slow. Molly glanced at the clock. She was going to miss her next class. It would just be a review of the readings from the last class, but she had questions about a couple of the articles. *Be present; worry later.*

"You're Carolyn, right?" Molly asked.

Carolyn nodded and took a deep breath then hiccupped.

"I'm sorry," she whispered.

"Don't be." Molly squeezed Carolyn one last time and stepped back. "There is no class here until noon, so take all the time you need."

"But we'll miss History of Social Work."

"So be it. I will explain to the professor."

Carolyn hiccupped again but sat on a nearby chair. Molly sat beside her.

"You don't need to say anything you don't want to. But I'm here to listen."

"When I was fo-fourteen I ran away from home. I was so mad at my parents; they wouldn't let me do anything." Carolyn wiped her face with her sleeve.

"I can imagine the rest of the story." Molly leaned forward, resisting the temptation to take off her mask.

Carolyn nodded and more of the tension left her.

"I was busted and because I was underage, social services returned me to my parents. They welcomed me, but I couldn't talk about what had happened. They acted like I'd never been gone, but it wasn't like home anymore. I didn't feel safe. I kept expecting my pimp to show up and drag me back to the street."

"I know the feeling." Molly put a hand on Carolyn's arm. "How did you manage the withdrawal?"

"I went to rehab and sorted out more than just the drugs. I'd liked them; they took me away from my dismal life. When I was high, I didn't mind the sex." Carolyn blushed deep red. "I couldn't go back to my old life like nothing had happened. I dropped out of band at school and didn't go to any of the parties or dances. Mom was ecstatic that I was finally working hard in school."

"And you let her believe that?"

"It was easier." Carolyn shrugged and took off her mask to wipe fresh tears from her face. "How could I tell her there were times I thought about running back to my pimp? Normal life – it was like I didn't fit in anymore. I couldn't talk to the boys, and the girls left me alone. I thought coming here would help, but it just made things worse. Everyone thinks I'm cold and aloof. Though I've gotten good grades, I don't feel like I'm learning anything."

Molly shoved her sleeve up and showed Carolyn the faint marks of needles on her arm. "These are my battle scars. They show I fought and won, but there are still nights I wake up shaking, wanting a fix."

"What do you do?" Carolyn's mouth dropped open.

"I talk to Blue, my dad, or I go to an NA meeting. Often both." Molly sighed and pulled her sleeve down. "When they say to take one day at a time, they aren't kidding. You can't change your past, and the future is in such flux that it's hard to think past this day, this moment."

"I wish I could do that." Heaving a great sigh, Carolyn pushed to her feet. Molly wrote her cell number on a scrap of paper.

"Call me if you need to talk." She handed the paper to Carolyn. "It isn't easy, but not many things that matter are."

Molly watched Carolyn walk out of the room, the weight of her world on her shoulders, then gathered her books.

"You did a good job." Professor Czysiki said behind Molly. She squeaked and spun around, dropping everything again.

"Sorry, but I felt I needed to stay in case you needed my help."

"I was desperately trying to keep her from crying again."

"Sometimes it's like that." The professor smiled wryly. "If you need to talk, drop by my office any time."

"I will." Molly picked up her books for the third time. "Professor Shin will be furious. This is the second class I've missed."

"I will talk to him and explain." Professor Czysiki handed Molly her History of Social Work text. "You go have a coffee and decompress."

"Thanks."

Molly walked out of the room and headed for the café. She wanted a coffee and time alone in the busyness of the other students. In the bright open space, time passed without her noticing. Until her History of Social Work professor showed up.

"Molly, you weren't in class." Professor Shin held up a hand. "My colleague explained the circumstances. Even as a history professor, I can see that some things take precedence over history lectures."

"I'm sorry, I had some questions I wanted to ask."

"Let me grab a coffee and you can ask them." Professor Shin smiled slightly.

"Thanks." Molly opened her text and tried to remember what had been burning questions earlier that morning.

## Chapter 2

Blue stretched and looked around at the organized chaos of the donations. He preferred being out on the street talking with people, but somehow he'd become a coordinator and stuck behind a desk most of the time.

A volunteer stuck their head into the back room where Blue worked. The dungeon as he thought of it. "Hey Blue, Judy wants to talk to you."

"Thanks, Hal." Blue stood up as his joints complained. If she wanted him to give up the two shifts a week on the street, he'd refuse. The chair was more dangerous than the people on the street. He put on his mask and walked through a room filled with people drinking coffee and eating a hot meal to the other side of the Loop. Waving at the nurses running the health clinic, he knocked on Judy's door and walked in.

She held up a hand.

"Are you sure?" She said into the phone.

"I see, very well."

Judy hung up.

"Blue, sit down." She waved at a chair. "Want a coffee?" Judy was already pouring two cups. "We have an opportunity which could be the greatest challenge the Loop has faced yet."

"Neighbours complaining again?" Blue could see their point but had little patience with the way they expressed their concerns.

"No more than usual."

"I told you, we should buy the house across the street and let them move on."

"Where is the four hundred thousand extra dollars in the budget? We can't buy out everyone who complains. For the moment, the city is tolerant of us; let's not rock the boat."

Blue looked over at the business license on the wall. Its existence had been under threat until Judy took the helm and made them look like a respectable agency. He missed the relaxed feel of the old days, but he had to admit knowing where and when their funding was coming in was a relief.

"Okay." Blue accepted the coffee and sat in the chair. He almost sighed. His usual chair was torturous.

"I have a proposition for you." Judy walked over and made sure the door was firmly shut before sitting down and steepling her fingers.

"Go on." The coffee tasted bitter, and he set it down.

"As part of the push to service street people more effectively," Judy didn't usually talk like that, so it had to be a quote from someone, probably the City, "We have been asked if we would be interested in sub-contracting to run something like The Loop downtown."

"Won't the 'optics' be even worse on the south shore?" Blue picked up his coffee so he could fiddle with the cup. "How many times were we almost closed because people didn't like what our work looked like?"

"You know I started at the end of that. We're hearing fewer complaints from a smaller group of people. Some of the store owners are even sending people our way."

"That's better than phoning the police. I wish they'd call the Peer Ambassadors more."

"Baby steps." Judy kept her gaze steady on Blue.

"Opening a downtown Loop is hardly a baby step."

"Which is why you are here." Judy smiled tightly. "I'm sorry to do this to you, but you're the only person both the board and I agree can manage the task."

"Thanks, I think." Blue sipped at cold coffee and made a face.

"I am aware that you prefer to be on the front lines on the street, but you are a highly effective manager. If this is going to work, we need someone like you at the helm."

"If I say no?" Blue's heart raced. The last thing he wanted was to be responsible for something as explosive as a new Loop location. Not when this one was still under a microscope.

"Then I will let the agency know that we are unable to help out at this time."

"And we will never get asked again." Blue ground his teeth. "Why can't you take it on?"

"The board wouldn't allow it." Judy's lips thinned. "They are already concerned about my workload. Having the Executive Director die of overload wouldn't look good."

"Right, they have a point." Blue put his cup down. "I would need to choose my own team."

"Bring a list to me and we will negotiate."

"Fair enough. When do we open?"

Judy grimaced. "At the beginning of the month."

"Not happening." Blue stood up. "I won't be the sacrificial goat. Find someone else to hang out to dry."

"Good." Judy leaned back. "I told them we could have a soft opening on the first of the month, but most of that month would be training and policy work."

Blue slowly sat down. "What would the job be? Managing the place is too vague."

Judy slid a file across the desk. "This details the nature of the project, the goals and objectives, and how we plan to measure them. I will be available for consultation. The agency has a liaison who will look after communication between you and the agency."

"Why do you keep saying 'the agency'? Which one?"

"Part of the reason they are sub-contracting us is to stay out of backlash."

"Of course."

"Tomorrow we can go look at the space and you can make requests about set up. The liaison will meet us there."

"You were pretty confident I was going to say yes." Blue rubbed his forehead, not sure whether to feel honoured or annoyed.

"It is easier to cancel at the last minute than to set something up at the last second."

"Right." Blue picked up the file and nodded at Judy before heading back to his desk. Maybe he could get a new chair as part of the bargain.

***

Blue rubbed his neck and closed the folder. He'd need to bring the Peer Ambassadors over to the downtown side of Kamloops and figure out how to get along with the Customer Care and Patrol Team . That would be the easy part. They'd have to get to know the neighbourhood and try to recruit people to fill out the teams. They had a system now which managed the worst of the 'optics' and left only a few hard-core complainers.

Then he needed people to staff the building itself. They had to come before he worried about the Peer Ambassadors. It would be a challenge to get people from the North Shore to travel downtown. Maybe he should offer bus passes to volunteers and staff both. It wasn't like there would be much parking space.

He'd have to adjust the system to match the new environment. What people should he ask for? Erica had been with the Peer Ambassadors since the first pilot project and had taken all the training and then some. She'd taken the course to become a certified Peer Counsellor. She worked in the Loop as a shift supervisor and had an effective group of people who tackled the more offensive graffiti.

*I need to see the place for myself.*

"I'm heading out to do some research." Blue waved at Genevieve as he left and walked toward the downtown.

The Overlander bridge was busy with traffic: cars, bikes, and pedestrians. Victoria Street West was less crowded, but people hung out in front of the Mustard Seed Mission and at the storage facility. Blue stopped to chat with a few of them. Some lost interest when he didn't produce money or smokes, but others latched onto him to spin endless stories of how life was treating them badly.

"The cops been watching for me and hassling me every time I put a foot on the street." Chas lifted a finger in the general direction of the passing traffic.

"It's tough to be known to the cops." Blue avoided pointing out that if Chas stopped fighting whenever he was on the street he'd get hassled less.

"Try hanging out at the Loop."

"Don't like the place; they keep throwing me out."

"That's because you started a fight. There are no fights allowed at the Loop. You aren't the only one asked to leave."

"Well, fuck you, too." Chas got up in Blue's face.

"Chill," one of the others said. "You bring the cops on us again, we'll kick the shit out of you."

Chas stomped off toward the Overlander bridge.

"Thanks." Blue waved at the group and wandered over to Victoria Street. He'd passed most of the downtown strip by the time he arrived where the new program would be run.

The place looked sad with windows covered by paper on the inside. Someone's dream had gone down the drain here. It might have been the location - too far off the main section of Victoria to gather much foot traffic and in the center of the block so parking would be an issue. He could see why they chose this spot to run their pilot program. A four-month project to evaluate the feasibility of a Loop-style service in the downtown area.

The proposal was half explanation of how the problems that arose on Tranquille wouldn't happen here. Blue snorted. He fully expected problems. The trick would be to prepare for them ahead of time. He dropped into the businesses closest to the site.

They had a different feel from the Tranquille strip. Maybe it was his imagination, but the people weren't as immediately suspicious when he pushed open the door. A few resisted his attempts at conversation, but he got his ear bent at a barber shop that looked like it had been there since Victoria was a dirt road.

It wasn't grimy, but it was worn. The linoleum on the floor had places the pattern had been worn off by decades of sweeping. The single barber looked like a garden gnome in a pinstripe suit. While Blue got an unnecessary haircut, the barber talked non-stop about how the neighbourhood had changed. He wasn't complaining, just telling history.

It was worth the ten bucks for the cut. Blue wandered out and half expected the street to be full of old cars. He shook his head and headed for home.

***

Cameron Robinson stopped Molly after class.

"You want to go out for drinks? As an apology for my stupid joke."

She had nothing against him, but the idea of going out with him made her skin crawl. It had the feel of being with a client, not a friend.

"Thanks, but no."

"Come on, it isn't like you're swamped with papers; we're in the same program after all."

"I didn't say I was busy. I said 'no.'" Molly couldn't keep the edge from her voice. "Is this going to be a problem?"

Robinson spun and walked away without answering.

# Chapter 3
### Thursday, September 7

A few days later, Blue met Judy and the liaison at the space.

"I was hoping for something a bit fresher looking." Blue peered at the wall which was an indeterminate grey. At least the place didn't smell, just a bit musty from not having the heat on full.

"It's what the budget can afford." Judy frowned at him and shook her head.

The liaison didn't appear to have heard him.

"I have some motivational posters in my office. They'll brighten the place up." *Maybe she'd heard after all.* "Call me Lee."

She wore what Blue would have expected to see at a business office, not a drop-in for street people. But then, they were just checking the place out. She pulled out a phone and made a note.

"I'm Blue." Blue half-reached out his hand to shake, but she didn't react to that or his name. Judy had probably told her, so the usual questions wouldn't be necessary. He prowled around while Lee ignored him and made more notes on her phone. Judy stood with a pained look on her face.

"The kitchen isn't up to code.," Blue said. "We won't be able to make much more than coffee without the health department complaining. I'd like some better seating too. Make the place look a bit more friendly."

Lee made a note. "We have some folding chairs that will do. Don't need a kitchen."

"I don't want it to look like we put the minimum amount of time and money into the project," Blue said emphatically

"It is only a four-month pilot." Lee stared at him.

"Do you want the pilot to succeed?" Blue frowned.

"Sure, I guess it would bring in more funding." Lee's forehead wrinkled. "But we can open a new place if it comes to that."

"Judy, this isn't going to work." Blue waved his hand at the empty room. "Count me out."

"Blue, wait." Judy held up a hand. "Lee, Blue is going to manage the project. He knows what he's talking about."

"Sure, the grant is for a peer-led centre, but the budget is a hundred thousand. We need to keep a tight grasp on accountability for spending." Lee waved a hand as if that was an unanswerable statement.

"Meaning you don't want the peers to know what is going on with the money." Blue headed for the door.

"Wait, you can't leave. The project has to be run by peers." Lee reached toward him, eyes wide.

Blue turned to face her. "Right then, I will manage the project, but I run it my way. I've read over the proposal. I need to see the budget. We'll get some proper furniture in here, make it welcoming. Some folks can scrub the walls. I'll talk to someone about the kitchen, see if we can get it certified without spending a mint."

"But—" Lee's eyes widened.

"You have a project intended to be run by peers. I can understand you wanting to keep an eye on things. You have accountability to the funder for starters. But your job is to get out of the way and let us do the work. If there's a problem, you and I talk about it and find a workable solution."

"The goals and objectives…"

"Yes, of course. That's why I needed to read the proposal and terms of reference for the project. How are you planning to measure the results of the pilot project?"

"Do you have an email? I'll send you the files." She pulled out the phone and made a note. "I suppose you won't need the motivational posters?"

Judy stood behind Lee with what, on anyone else, he would have called a smirk on her face.

"Not just yet," Blue said, then took pity on the woman. "They will be useful for the staff."

"Staff…" Lee sighed. "…of course, you will want to hire your own staff."

"Since you know the project better, I would like your input on the interviews." Blue rubbed his shoulder. "I'm not saying I intend to ignore you completely, but if I'm to do this, then I need to be more than a token peer."

"I think I get it." Lee shook her head. "Let's meet after you've gone through the paperwork."

"Sounds like a plan." Blue smiled. "I will get on to setting the place to rights."

***

"I wish I could have been the fly on the wall," Molly giggled and flopped lazily on the couch in their living room. Harley lay on the floor and rolled on her back, looking for a scratch.

"I don't think she imagined dealing with a peer who could talk in her own language." Blue shrugged.

"After three years of me being in the Social Work program, you must have picked up some of the lingo." Molly pointed at him. "Next thing you'll be the executive director."

"Don't say that!" Blue shuddered theatrically. "I'd never get out from behind the desk again."

Molly only laughed harder. "I'll start dinner; you set the table." She sliced up a chicken breast and stir fried it with vegetables from the fridge. While she cooked, she wondered what Blue would make of the situation at the Community Social Work class. Carolyn had missed several classes of Community Social Work, but Molly had seen the girl from a distance in the café and at other courses during the week. Maybe she was embarrassed at her breakdown, but skipping classes in fourth year wasn't good.

"There's a girl in one of my classes I'm worried about." Molly set the pan on the pad on the table. "Dig in."

"Looks good." Blue filled his plate and tucked in. "I'm a much more basic cook."

Molly ate slowly. Blue would respond when he was ready.

"What kind of worry?" Blue took seconds of the stir-fry. "Afraid she's suicidal or just doing poorly?"

"I've seen her around, but she hasn't been in class since my presentation for Community Social Work."

"Maybe it hit a little close to home." Blue glanced up at Molly. "You mentioned you slipped up and got personal."

"She did hang on to me and weep." Molly restrained the impulse to tell Carolyn's story. "What she talked about is confidential. She might just be embarrassed."

"Why don't you see if she shows up this week."

"I guess." Molly's gut said something was off, but Blue was right. All she could do was wait.

"What do you want to do for the weekend?"

"Someone was raving about the waterfalls in Wells Gray Park. It reminded me I haven't checked out Peterson Creek recently. The weather is supposed to clear and cool. A hike might help clear my head."

"Wish I could come, but I have to review the proposal and budget for a meeting on Monday."

"That's what comes of being unexpectedly competent."

"I should have kept my mouth shut."

"As if," Molly laughed. "You'll make that pilot project such a success they will have no choice but to keep it going."

"That would be nice, but grants are more for new programs than old ones. Funding is going to be an issue."

"That's four months away. Focus on what is in front of you."

"What's in front of me is dinner." Blue turned his concentration to his plate.

***

## Sunday, September 11

Molly followed the Peterson trail up from downtown through the park to the waterfall. She needed to get her heart rate up to distract her from the bit of worry that refused to leave her stomach. After walking up and down paths, she stopped thinking about anything but what was in front of her. Up ahead a black shape walked out of the brush and looked straight at Molly.

The bear wasn't very big and looked too cute for her to be scared, but where there was a little one, there might be a mother bear. She didn't know that much about them beyond the occasional articles in the paper about parks being closed because of a bear.

The bear looked away and walked across the path. Molly turned and headed back down. A group of young men were walking toward her. They were being loud enough that she doubted the bear would bother them. She took a side track to go around them.

A hand landed roughly on her shoulder. Molly's judo training kicked in as she twisted and threw the person hard on the ground.

"Shit." Robinson, the joker from her presentation, lay glaring up at her. "I just wanted to ask if you wanted to grab coffee sometime. No hard feelings."

"You asked me out and I said 'no'." Molly looked at Robinson's friends standing with gaping mouths. *Idiots.* "Do you always ask a girl out by grabbing her from behind?"

"Sorry." He winced as he pushed himself to his feet. "Did you learn that from your pimp?"

Molly's stomach became ice. She wanted to throw him down the hill into the creek. "Be careful, there is a bear further up the path."

"You think I should be afraid of some bear?" Robinson's flushed face made her wonder if he was on some kind of drug.

"I wouldn't want the poor thing to get indigestion from attacking you." Molly snapped her mouth closed on the rest of what she wanted to say and turned to walk away.

"Don't walk away from me, you ho." Sounds of a struggle behind her suggested his friends had stepped in to keep him from coming after her.

"Chill, dude," one said. "Do you *want* to get tossed again?"

Molly didn't hear the reply.

The ice in her belly had melted by the time she made it downtown to catch the bus home. He was an ass, not the first and probably not the last she'd have to deal with.

By the time she'd gotten home, a brisk shower was all she needed to put him out of her mind.

Blue was deep into paperwork, and Molly didn't want to sit around idly, letting her mind focus on the incident. She called her adopted niece, Ciara, to see what the younger girl was doing.

"Nothing. I'm grounded." Ciara didn't sound at all chastened.

"What did you do this time?"

"Snuck out to go to a party."

"And I bet there was drinking there."

"You sound like Grandma."

"I know from experience where that can lead." Molly closed her eyes and pushed the memories away.

"Really?" Ciara said sarcastically.

"I'm coming over to visit your grandma. If I happen to see you, we'll have a talk."

Ciara had been walking on a precipice since her mother died of an overdose. She was less willing to listen to her grandmother. Molly had shifted from being the cool aunt to just another adult who didn't understand.

The bus ride to the Reserve and the walk to Ciara's house gave Molly lots of time to imagine horrible things happening to the bright young girl.

"Come in." Hanna looked up to where rap music blared from Ciara's room. "I'm not sure which of us is being punished."

"Let me talk to her."

"Be my guest. I'll have the first aid kit ready to dress your wounds."

Molly laughed and walked up the stairs to knock on Ciara's door.

"Come in."

Molly walked in to gangster rap playing at full volume. She looked at the speakers but didn't say anything. Ciara's chin was set stubbornly.

The lyrics flowed over Molly like a landslide of muck and anger.

"Do you think people who do you wrong should be shot? That women are only valuable for sex?"

"No. I like the rhythm." Ciara turned off the music and sat on the bed, her arms crossed.

"There is Indigenous rap. The Halluci Nation is a big one. The rhythm doesn't have to be accompanied by gangster rap."

"Like you'd know."

"Do you rap?"

"Nah, nobody wants to listen to me."

"You'd be good at it."

"You think?" Ciara's eyes lit up for a second. "It doesn't matter. The kids at school would just laugh at me. I haven't had to survive on the streets."

"I'd be a terrible rapper," Molly said. "You remember when we first met?"

"What, you're going to tell me what a sweet young child I was?"

"At a party when I was your age then, I was assaulted the first time." Molly stared out the window. "I'd been groped and stuff before; I thought it was just part of life. But that time it hurt. I wanted to scream."

"Why didn't you?"

"I didn't think anyone would care." Molly ignored the tears on her cheeks. "I was just a foster brat; I probably deserved it."

"Nobody deserves that." Ciara handed Molly a tissue.

"By the time I was your age, I was turning tricks for spending money. It was the only thing I was good for. Touch was for sex or a beating. Then I met Blue, and I freaked out. I couldn't understand him. He didn't want anything from me. I went to a treatment centre. It took most of a year for me to understand it wasn't about me being worthless. Life was supposed to be kind. I had a hard time with that."

Ciara wrapped her arms around Molly and held her tight. "You don't have to tell me this."

"When I say I'm worried about you, I'm not thinking about you having a beer or making out. I'm thinking about my life and how awful I'd feel if that happened to you."

"I'm sorry," Ciara sobbed. "I didn't know."

"You shouldn't have to know." She stroked Ciara's back. "I worry about your life being taken from you. Make your own decisions but make wise ones."

"I'll try." Ciara sniffled.

"It's hard, I know, but I will always be here to talk. Doesn't matter how bad you think you've been. I'll hold you until you remember you are loved."

"Thanks, Molly." Ciara sat up and blew her nose. "God, I'm a mess."

"I'm no better." Molly laughed. "Let's put ourselves back together, then have tea with your grandma.

# Chapter 4

**Monday, September 12**

Volunteers from the Loop scrubbed at the walls, revealing a less grimy grey. Contractors were discussing the kitchen.

"I can hardly believe it." Lee looked around at the bustling people in the new Loop. The air smelled of strong cleaners and coffee.

"We are used to doing things on our own." Blue poured himself a cup. "We ran a four-month program with less than thirty thousand dollars. Everyone pulled together. There were problems, but there always will be."

Lee looked around and shook her head. "I wouldn't believe it if I weren't watching. You'd never see this at my agency."

"Like many others, you see clients. I see an accountant, a truck driver, a plumber. We look at peers who may need a hand up. People respond to that and start believing they aren't trash. That changes things from us helping them to them helping each other." Blue chuckled and shook his head. "It is still like herding cats, but I think it should be. We have to decide to help and be helped, and that can be hard."

Blue held up a hand. "But we didn't meet so I could preach at you. I have a few questions about the budget. The administrative fee I understand, but the project is being charged for you to work half-time. That is probably because you took liaison to mean coordinator. Since it is the agency charging us, so I expect if you suddenly had time to fill, there would be no problem finding work for you. I'd like to cut that to ten hours a week and use the rest to supplement what we pay the staff."

"I think we can do that. I'd have to talk to my supervisor." Lee made a note on her phone. "The proposal calls for two staff from nine to five, Monday to Friday."

"We should have at least three people on-site at all times we're open, more during peak times."

"You think we'll need that?" Lee looked at him doubtfully. Conversation from the cleaning crew floated over.

"Everybody has issues, and they'll bring them in that door. Overdose, psychotic breaks, anger at a fight from last week. We'll see them all and deal with them. Safety demands we have backup on site. Sure, we could call the police, but that should be a last resort, not the first reaction." Blue shook himself. "Training started last week and continues through the project. Helping the community is your goal for the pilot. Mine is using this time to build capacity in the community."

"You should be a social work professor." Lee cupped her cup with her hands. "I'm learning more than I did at my degree."

"They gave you a toolbox. Now you are being asked to open it up and put scratches on the tools."

"Right."

"My daughter says sometimes I talk too much." Blue drained his coffee and put the mug on a table. "Let me introduce you to the core team members. We'll do the whole interview thing later. I know these people are hard workers and able to handle crisis upon crisis. Most of them won't work anything like full time so we'll have a bigger staff than you accounted for."

He led Lee over to the cleaning crew.

"This is the boss?" A woman who could have been anything from thirty to sixty years of age peered at her doubtfully.

"No." Lee nodded at Blue. "He's the boss. I'm here to help make sure everything works smoothly and report to my supervisor on what we're learning. I'm Lee."

"Erica." She looked at Blue "They're really letting you run this thing?"

"So I'm told," Blue said. "How's the cleaning coming?"

"'Bout what you'd expect. Had to review the MSDS with 'em. Convince 'em that the gloves and goggles weren't just for looks."

"MS what?" Lee wondered if she'd fallen down some rabbit hole. Since she'd met Blue, the simple straightforward project had twisted and turned, giving her mental whiplash.

"Material Safety Data Sheets. Tells ye what precautions you need to handle shit safely." Erica rolled her eyes. "We'll be doing WHMIS training. Workplace Hazardous Material Information Sheets. You can sit in.

"Everyone here was something before they experienced homelessness," Blue said. "That knowledge hasn't vanished."

"Of course." Lee looked around the room and tried to imagine what the people working on the building might have done before their lives fell apart.

***

"During this term and the next, you will be placed with various organizations," Professor Huston said. "The goal will be to experience the diverse kinds of social work and programs. This course is graded pass/fail, but don't assume it is lax. Attendance is mandatory unless you have the permission of your supervisor and a plan to make up the lost time. Keep an open mind."

Molly's placement was with a small group working on a housing project which had been ongoing for several years. *Should be interesting enough.*

"Want to trade?" Carolyn waved her envelope. "I got stuck with some lame thrift shop."

"If the professor okays it, I don't mind." Molly gathered her courage. "How are you doing? I was worried when you missed class."

"I dropped the course; it isn't what I expected. I'm taking Clinical instead." Carolyn waved a hand.

"As long as you're good."

"Why wouldn't I be?" Carolyn's eyes held a challenge. Molly didn't rise to the bait.

"Let's ask the prof about trading."

Somehow things got turned around, so it sounded like Molly was the one asking for the switch, but the prof sighed and said, "That's fine, but learning is learning, Ms. Callister. The easier your assignment, the harder it will be to write the paper."

Molly took the bus down to Seymour and found the thrift shop. A woman named Agatha ran the till. She sat hunched behind the counter, a cane leaning against the wall in easy reach. The store was crowded with clothes, dishes, and other oddities.

"The owner put in the application. I didn't expect them to actually send someone. Sorry, I don't really have a plan for you. Maybe sort some of the

33

clothes in the back. Dale is back there. He looks scary, but if you don't show fear, you'll be fine."

Molly walked to the back not sure if she was going to find a dog or a person. It turned out to be an exceptionally large cat. It hissed at Molly from the top of a pile of clothes. Molly shrugged and started sorting out the clothes worth selling and the stuff no one in their right mind would wear. She had to put in a minimum of sixty hours over the term, then write a paper to present to the class. It could be a long two months. Then they would do it again in the new year.

After she'd finished the clothes on the table. Molly explored the back room, finding every size and shape of human clothing. She tried on a green leather jacket before wistfully putting it back.

"Looks good on you." Agatha leaned against the door.

"But you could sell it."

"Think of it as a perk of the job. It's time for tea." Agatha led the way, thumping her cane, to the corner of the back room where a tiny table and two chairs were set beside a mattress.

She plugged in a kettle and put a tea bag in an old brown teapot.

"It's not much but it's home."

"You live here?"

"Couldn't afford rent anymore, got cut off disability 'cause I can't find a doctor to fill out the form. I'm on a waiting list, so maybe next year."

"That's terrible."

"Plenty in worse shape." Agatha poured the boiling water into the pot. "I write letters to the government and city council but never get a response. Enough of that, or it will spoil the tea."

Molly drank her weak black tea while the leather jacket seemed to get heavier with each sip. "What would you price this jacket at?"

"Likely twenty bucks, and someone will steal it." Agatha shrugged. "The owner rents the place to me cheap enough I can keep the wolf from the door. She turns a blind eye to my pad here. Lives in Vancouver in a fancy condominium. She complains about the fees. I think having the store here is cheaper than paying people to watch it."

They finished their tea undisturbed and went back to work. Molly sorted clothes on automatic trying to think of some way to help Agatha without being obvious.

*Maybe Blue will have a suggestion.* She phoned him to see if he had time for coffee.

***

They met at the Vic after she'd said goodbye to Agatha.

"Hard day?" Blue asked as she sat down.

"First day of placement." Molly had left the leather jacket behind. Her conscience wouldn't allow her to keep it. At least not without finding a way to help Agatha. She explained the situation while Blue drank his coffee.

"Think about it as a social worker." He said when she was done. "What agencies might be able to help? How do you get them involved?"

"You're right." Molly leaned back and sipped at her tepid coffee. "I can't help someone without them wanting to be helped. I'll do some research and talk to Agatha."

"You might want to prepare yourself to be rebuffed. Not everyone wants help."

***

"Your friend would need to be VATed, that is be interviewed to determine their vulnerability to homelessness and what priority they would get services. If she were presently living on the street, or about to be, she'd be a higher priority."

"There's a wait list for the geared-to-income apartments. Put her name on, but it could be a year or more before she gets a chance. There is a plan to build more units next year; that might shorten the wait."

"Does she have any mental health issues? You could refer her for counselling."

Molly wanted to pull her hair out. Agatha needed to be in desperate straits to get immediate help. Even the minimal amount of precarious housing and income she had put her far down the list. Agatha didn't seem to be immediately concerned; as long as the thrift store stayed open, she'd scrape by.

The next two days passed with myriad pinpricks of irritation. Her phone vanished for a day, then she found it in her bag, battery drained. Robinson leered at her when no one was watching. His first name was Cam, but Molly didn't want to humanize him that much. Several of her classmates asked her about rumours she was great in bed. Apparently, some old client had said so.

"The notion that sex workers are somehow experts in fucking is nonsense. Most of them fake what little response they have. The clients are pathetic. There is good reason many workers are addicts. I can recommend several books on the subject if you are interested." Molly didn't even try to take the scathing edge from her voice.

She was sure Robinson was behind the rumours, but without any proof, there was nothing she could do except avoid the café and practice her glare. The other students took to keeping their distance. She refused any offers to meet for coffee for fear she'd be propositioned.

Then she'd misread the question on a paper for History of Social Work and ended up staying up all night to rewrite it.

By the time she was to work for Agatha again, the thrift shop was looking like a retreat.

In the meantime, she worked off her irritation by walking Harley who didn't mind the extra attention at all. The dog was an excellent listener as she talked about her worries.

***

Blue noticed Molly was quieter than usual, but she'd talk to him when she was ready. He had his own concerns as the news of the new centre got out and everyone who had missed all the previous stories about it got upset.

There was a brief demonstration by the café with people protesting the criminal element that they claimed would be attracted to the centre. They waved signs.

*Stop Crime!*
*No gathering of criminals.*

A handful of people walked in circles chanting. Since the centre hadn't opened yet, the only people inconvenienced were the shop owners and those wanting to shop.

When Blue moved around the crowd to unlock the door and enter, a tall man put his hand on the door, holding it closed.

"You can't have a place for addicts and criminals here."

"Please remove your hand." Blue kept his voice gentle and quiet.

"I will not let you ruin this neighbourhood, too."

"If you are going to yell in my face, please put on a mask."

"Masks?" the man shouted. "Why should I hide my face? I'm not ashamed of my opinion."

A siren whooped and the demonstrators who had been crowding Blue stepped back.

"Officer, this man is harbouring criminals."

"Morning, Constable Post."

"What's going on, Blue?" the big cop ignored the sputtering man.

"Different day, same shit." Blue opened the door. "They were getting between me and my work. Just got a little excited and forgot that they can't block the sidewalk. No harm done."

He walked inside and locked the door. Lee stood pale-faced with her cell phone clutched in her hand.

"You alright?" He looked back out the door where the tall man was shouting at the cop. The rest of the protesters had vanished.

"I thought they were going to mob you."

"I expected most were too smart for that. Just a bit of inconvenience. If they're out there when you leave or arrive, go out the back or call me."

Blue's phone rang.

"Blue."

"Not what I'd call trouble, Judy. The fuss over the Loop on the North Shore got more than a little ugly before it settled down. I expect this will blow over too." He hung up and looked around. "Erica knows how to get people jumping. The place looks much better."

"She said she was bringing some art for the walls."

"Good. I don't want distractions keeping us from opening."

His phone buzzed and he checked the text.

[Have a look at this. I've already been banned.]

Blue tapped on the link from Naomi.

**Citizens for a Crime-Free Kamloops**

JB [these places only pander to the criminal element. When the Loop on Tranquille was open, the crime on the street went through the roof.]

KH [We need more security on the streets. The only thing the cops do is give them a slap on the wrist.]

JB [These people need to be locked up. What are our courts doing? Just toss them in prison, then they'll have a home.]

AR [Our streets are full of addicts wandering with their piles of trash. No wonder crime is up.]

He texted her back. [Let them rant, better on Facebook than on the street.]

The news talked about a group that wanted to build affordable housing in Rayleigh, despite all the services being in Kamloops. Probably without talking to anyone in Rayleigh either.

He wished that people would stop trying to attack homelessness and start working to deal with the underlying causes. Lazy was a label often thrown at people who were homeless, but it took more than a bit of hard work to get off the streets. The simplest solution was the one most often ignored. Money. The wrong people had most of it.

Blue shook his head and went to check on the kitchen. Everything looked in order. By the time he was finished, Erica had arrived with more workers carrying art. She supervised its hanging, making the space look more like a café than an empty store front.

"I have a line on some tables and chairs. Ron can pick them up and bring them here."

"Sounds good; maybe bring them in through the back. In fact, keep most of the traffic in and out through the back for now."

***

"So how's work at the thrift shop? Any good clothes?" Carolyn sidled up to Molly.

"The usual stuff, a few gems for people who look hard enough. The woman who runs the place has an enormous cat in the back. I'm not sure what the learning will be, but I'm getting pretty good at sorting the clothes.

"The housing thing is just one boring meeting after another. Government grant this, zoning that. I should have stuck with the thrift shop; I might have scored some nice vintage clothing."

"Probably, why don't you come by the place and have a look."

As if Carolyn talking to Molly was a signal, other students gathered around to brag or commiserate about their placements and soon the feeling of isolation was gone. A group of them took the bus down to the shop after their last class for the day. Molly showed them around. She'd expected Agatha to be pleased, but the woman wouldn't come out from behind her counter and frowned as if the students moving through the store were a nuisance.

"What's up with the old biddy?" Carolyn whispered.

"I don't know." Molly shrugged. "I only met her the one time, maybe she's normally like this."

"You have my condolences."

The crowd left and Molly approached Agatha, shocked to see tears on the woman's cheeks.

"What's wrong?"

"The owner is selling the place. Got an offer from a developer she couldn't refuse. I have to close up, and someone is coming to empty the store next month." Agatha slumped in her chair. "What will I do? Dale will be so upset."

"That's terrible." Molly's belly burned as she clenched her jaw. "There must be something we can do."

"Nah, the world don't care. What's one more old lady on the street?"

"I can try to get you help."

"No." Agatha straightened and poked a finger at Molly. "I won't be sneered at and pitied by the people at those agencies."

"At least let me finish out my placement. Maybe we can come up with something."

"You're sweet, but I'm not holding my breath. The world isn't kind to people like me."

"City Hall is going to build new housing, maybe we can petition them to speed up the process."

Agatha laughed. "City Hall can't do anything. It's the provincial and federal folks holding up the process with their penny-pinching. All they can do is make noise."

"We could make noise, too."

"Won't matter, election is coming up. Nobody will be thinking of anything but winning."

"I'll make homelessness an election issue." Molly insisted. "At least it is something."

"I won't be the poor lady drug through the news as the sad case. I'd rather run for office than go through that."

"Why don't you?"

"Why don't I do what?"

"Run for office." Molly sat on the counter. "What better way to make housing an issue?"

Agatha roared with laughter. "Wouldn't that put a wrench in their spokes? Why not? I haven't been a mayor in decades."

"You were mayor?" Molly stared at Agatha.

"In a tiny place called Spruce Bay. Mine closed and most folks bailed out of town. I was the only one fool enough to get run for the job. Haven't thought of that place in ages."

44

"Do we have time to get you nominated?" Molly pulled out her phone and did a quick search. "We have a few days to get the papers in. You need twenty-five signatures."

"I'll have a buck a bag sale and get folks to sign. It will be fun. The stuff will all go to the dump anyway. I have one condition." Agatha pointed to the green leather jacket. "You wear that home."

"Okay, if you insist." Molly picked it up and put it on. "I will be here after school is over to see how you're doing."

# Chapter 5
## Thursday, September 15

"I'm not sure now is the best time to have a homelessness issue-driven campaign." Blue sat at the kitchen table and rubbed his forehead. "The new centre is already getting backlash from some parts of the community."

"Agatha wants to do it, and I'm going to help her." Molly didn't know why she was reacting more like Ciara than a reasonable adult.

"Fine, but try to keep me and the new centre out of the limelight."

"We won't ask you for a recommendation. We'll be running the campaign from the thrift shop."

"What about school?"

"I can manage my courses and the campaign for one month."

"As long as you're sure." Blue sighed. "I don't know why this has got my stomach in a knot."

"The City is managing the funding for the new centre, right?" Molly put her hand on his shoulder. "I promise I'll keep the centre out of the campaign."

"See that you do."

Molly closed her eyes and breathed deeply. "I will." She packed her books and headed for the bus up to TRU. Life used to be simple. If there was a problem, she and Blue talked about it, and it went away, or at least begin to. He was getting busier with the Loop and now the new centre. He had his own problems, ones she couldn't help with. Her problems were her own. She'd just have to deal with them one way or another.

She got off the bus and walked to class. The other students didn't avoid her, but they made no move to join her. It was Robinson's turn to present on working with a specific group or community. He talked about a project in Ireland where two Canadians had set up a hockey league and mixed Catholics and Protestants on the teams. Barriers broke down and tensions relaxed. It was interesting and something she'd never considered. Sports as community intervention? How would that work here in Kamloops? The biggest divide was across class lines. The people on the upper side had all the sports they could want.

Social Work History was next. They talked about the formation of social work groups and standards, making social work a profession, and events leading to many of the standards and ethics they were learning at the university.

Robinson came over to her in the café and her stomach clenched.

"How about I buy you supper as an apology for my behaviour?"

"Thanks, but I will accept your apology without supper."

"You think I'm a lunatic out to get you? I have a girlfriend, who is already pissed that I'm even asking you."

"You should listen to your girlfriend," Molly said. "I don't have anything against you, but I don't feel any need to get to know you better either."

His face clouded and he stomped off. She'd lied to him. He made her nervous; the few times they'd interacted felt off. Maybe it was just her, but she wasn't going to ignore the feeling.

Butterflies invaded her stomach on the ride down to the thrift shop. What would she find? More despair at the unfairness of life? Whatever, it would distract her from Robinson. Maybe he was a nice guy who just made a couple of mistakes, but what if he wasn't?

The shop looked much barer than when she'd left the day before. A few women picked through the racks. Agatha sat behind the counter surrounded by paperwork. An ancient button maker sat to the side and a box of the pieces it needed on the floor.

"Could you go bring out more clothes, dear?" Agatha looked up for a second, then returned to the papers.

Molly went to the back and dragged out a rack of sorted clothes and started figuring out where to put them in the store. The women shoppers helped her out. Two of them wore buttons saying, 'Agatha for Mayor.'

Once the rack was emptied, she started sorting clothes.

"You know what's going on, Dale?" She asked the cat, but it didn't respond aside from parking itself on the pile she was working on.

That became the rhythm of the day. Sort, bring out clothes, go back and sort more. By the time Agatha put the *closed* sign on the door, Molly had worked herself into an almost trance.

"That will do, Molly," Agatha called from the door. "Time for tea and a council of war."

Molly dropped the jeans she was holding and went up front.

"These are the nomination forms. I have the signatures I need and then some. The other stuff is about fundraising and advertising. We have to keep good records, or we'll get in trouble with Elections BC."

"Right." Molly looked through them. Agatha had already filled out some parts. The guide was a ninety-two-page PDF. "You have me down as your financial officer."

"Should be easy enough. Donations under $50 can be anonymous. We aren't going to spend much on advertising. I'll help you with it."

"I guess." Molly took a sip of her tea. *What have I got myself into?* She filled out her information, cringing a bit at the penalties for failing to report.

"Tomorrow morning I'll file the papers at City Hall. We'll be a day or two ahead of the cut-off."

Molly caught the bus home. She'd imagined handing out flyers or the like. This was way past that, but since it was her idea, she'd figure it out. It couldn't be worse than statistics.

At home, Blue was in the bedroom with the door shut, which usually meant he was on the phone with Kelly. Harley lay on her bed but lifted her head to woof at Molly.

"C'mon, Harley, let's go for a walk." Molly fetched the leash and led the dog out of the apartment.

They walked down to Schubert and the Rivers Trail. She did her best thinking while walking along the river.

"Maybe I've been depending on Blue too much. He has his own life, and it's complicated enough. He says they're fine with being friends, but I wonder if that is how Kelly really feels. It's their life, so they'll have to sort it out. I wish Kelly would visit, aside from the attempted murder and stuff, it was fun. I still have that card from the security guy. I don't know why; I'm going to be a social worker like Grandma."

As they approached the Overlander Bridge, Harley didn't quite growl, but her hackles were up.

"Let's turn around and head home. I don't need any more trouble." She doubted there was anything short of a grizzly Harley couldn't handle even with only three legs.

A black bear poked its nose out of the brush. Not a very big one. It vanished when Harley growled. The walk back was quiet, though she found herself watching for more bears. Didn't matter this was the first bear she'd ever seen on the trail.

Back at the apartment she sighed and dropped on the couch. Blue's door was open, so the call was done.

"Feel better?" Blue came out of the kitchen with plates of mac and cheese. "It doesn't rival yours, but it's edible."

They sat to eat, and the silence slipped from being uncomfortable to being familiar. She started washing the dishes when they were done.

"How was your day?" Blue asked.

"School went well enough. Agatha is having a ball. She's going to file the paperwork tomorrow. Apparently, I'm the financial officer for the campaign. It will be a learning experience."

"You are allowed to say no." Blue scratched Harley behind the ears.

"I did say no today, to supper with a guy who creeps me out a little."

"Creepy doesn't go well with supper."

"Maybe I'm not being fair to him; he is trying to apologize." Molly put the last dish on the rack.

"That doesn't obligate you to accept invitations." Blue swivelled to look at her. "Trust your gut. Better to turn down an innocent invitation than get caught up in something dangerous."

"True." Molly flopped on the couch. "So true."

***

**Friday, September 17**

"We should pull the plug." Judy paced around the café. "That twit John Brown has the happenings at the demonstration twisted to make us at fault. It's overflowing onto the Loop.

"Of course, he does." Blue leaned against a table. "He isn't going to admit that he messed up. Better to suggest a conspiracy between the police and the Loop. Never mind that we are sub-contracted to the agency. I won't let policy be dictated by flame wars on Facebook."

"It isn't your decision, Blue," Judy sighed.

"You made me manager; the agency agreed. If you pull the plug, I'm quitting. It doesn't sit right being the token peer. I expect you will lose Erica and a few others who have put a lot of time into this project."

"There is pressure from the City."

"What a surprise." Blue widened his eyes. "The City has a habit of running for cover at the first sign of trouble. Remember the whole 'optics' fiasco a couple years back?"

"We did a lot of backpedalling, Blue."

"We found leverage and used it. Now the Loop is accepted by most of the businesses. They invited us to join the BIA, for Pete's sake."

"I'm sure that was a mistake." Judy frowned at him, then chuckled. "We should have accepted just to see their faces."

"It was going to be me attending the meetings. No thanks."

"The news has picked up the story."

"Alleged this, alleged that. The RCMP refuses to comment. We should return fire."

"We can't sink to their level."

"We don't; we rise above it and provide facts. Ignore the bullshit and talk about the good this place is going to do. Get in the papers, on the radio, make them look the raving lunatics they are."

"I will leave it up to you then."

***

"The centre will be properly staffed, and I will be on-site during open hours. We have a grant to do this run by peers. What is going to be the fallout if we get shut down before we even started? You think the funder will send any more money our way?" Blue kept his voice level and reasonable. They sat in the sound booth in the lobby of CBC Radio on Victoria

"The city is the one controlling the funds," the CBC reporter said.

"Yes, they are the community entity, but the money is from the provincial government. Are they going to send back the money they've already spent? It is like the City tearing up a road to fix it, then stopping in the middle because of complaints about the dust. It is important to look at the long-term goal. That is to provide a safe place for people to drop in during the day. Living on the street is both desperation and boredom. We alleviate the boredom; we alleviate the desperation. We alleviate the desperation; we begin to address the issues around street crime."

"So you are saying that street crime is a problem."

"Of course, it is a problem. Our position is that the crime is attributable to a small portion of people on the street. Just like not every member of any group is the same as the worst members."

"You're saying there are law-abiding, tidy homeless people?"

"Yes, but you don't see them because they are tidy, law-abiding people who can't find an apartment they can afford. The vacancy rate is still under three percent, less than that for affordable housing. Homelessness is not a crime, but that it still exists in this day and age is criminal."

"Thank you, that was Blue, the manager of the yet-to-be-named centre on Victoria Street. Now for the weather…"

Blue slipped out of the booth and was met by the producer.

"Thanks for coming in. It was a good interview."

***

## Citizens for a Crime-Free Kamloops

OG [Did you hear the interview with this Blue guy? He basically said treat scum nicely and they'll become responsible citizens.

JB  [Who is this Blue? I did some digging and learned he's been involved in criminal activities before. Who's to say he isn't already selling drugs out of that place?]

Mod    [Please    refrain    from    making unsupportable accusations. We don't want this forum shut down.]

JB [Are you one of them? Can nobody—] *User banned.*

# Chapter 6
## Tuesday, September 22

Molly had barely begun the campaign, and she was already drowning in paper. It covered the table she'd been sorting clothes on. Dale was annoyed at the lack of soft piles to sleep on. There were receipts for every donation, piles separating donations that didn't count as expenses from those that did. The information from opening the bank account for the campaign took its own corner.

Fortunately, Agatha had a good idea of how it worked, at least in a small, northern town. It remained to be seen how that translated to Kamloops. There were three contenders for mayor who had been on the last council. The incumbent had retired, so it was an open race. Then there was John Brown and Agatha Howard.

She figured the first challenge would be to get the media to pay attention to them. There was already an 'and also' feel to the reporting. It didn't help that Agatha's official biography leapt over twenty years from Spruce Bay to the present as the proprietor of a thrift shop.

"Don't worry about it," Agatha told her. "What we do going forward is what matters."

"Only if people know about it."

"Oh, they'll know." Agatha chuckled and Molly shivered.

At least the paperwork could be done between classes, but she'd had to put her phone on silent to keep from disturbing the professors and other students.

"It is such a great human-interest story, a homeless woman running for mayor of a major city," one reporter gushed. Molly wanted to point out that she had a home, sort of, for a while at least. Instead, she answered questions and tried to get some of Agatha's policy statements out there.

And boy, were they out there. Agatha had her look up the Wikipedia page for French anarchist Pierre-Joseph Proudhon. "Property is Theft" was the only clear statement about his theory.

Agatha's version was that the process of buying up property for the sole purpose of renting it out was theft. That property could have been purchased by an individual who is now forced to pay rent which not only paid for the cost of the property but provided a profit.

Molly had a tough time getting her head around that too. Agatha's bringing up Berlin's take over of more than ten thousand apartments from corporations to reduce the cost of rent didn't make her life easier.

John Brown was running on an anti-crime platform. All agencies working with the poor should be closed and the money used to build institutions to house the indigent. He didn't use those exact terms, but that was the gist. The housing crisis would be solved, and the people would be easier to police. He wanted to streamline the court system to get criminals to jail more efficiently.

"Don't worry, it will work out in the All-Candidates Meetings," Agatha declared cheerfully, but the first All-Candidates Meeting came and went without either Agatha or Mr. Brown being invited. Molly got her fellow students to push a petition stating that all candidates should be invited or it was neither a fair nor democratic election.

The organizers apologized, but it was still a blow to the campaign.

Robinson kept pestering her. He wanted to help with the campaign, he was really a nice guy, she should give him a chance. She kept her answers short. No. Probably. No.

He reminded her of a john who had an unhealthy crush on one of the girls. Desperate and more than a little sad. As an added insult, someone had stolen her green leather coat. Agatha would be upset.

Carolyn was a great help with designing and printing brochures. Molly carefully counted Carolyn's time as a donation and the brochures as an expense. A student had hired her to create a business card and better safe than sorry.

One night when Molly worked late with Carolyn, the other girl insisted on driving Molly home. She even insisted on walking Molly to the door.

"There are too many creeps around these days," Carolyn said.

"Don't you know it." Molly punched in her number and pulled the door open. She ran up the stairs to the apartment where Harley greeted her with enthusiasm.

***

Molly went with Agatha as she walked up and down Victoria Street wearing a purple coat with an oversized "Agatha for Mayor" button talking with anyone who stopped.

"Hi, I'm Agatha Howard. I'm running for mayor. What issues concern you?"

"You're that nut that says rent is theft." One man stopped and pointed at her.

"That's right, though it is more complicated than that. When corporations buy up land and houses for the sole purpose of renting to people for a profit, they aren't adding value to the land. They're simply holding the people who need homes hostage. 'Pay our rent or be homeless.'"

"That isn't how it works. The companies build the apartments, that's value added." The man rolled his eyes.

"True enough, if the land isn't already being used. But even then, they leave a solid margin for profit, or they wouldn't be renting. Then there are the old buildings that barely meet code anymore. The rent goes up, but the building isn't different. But here I am rattling on when I want to know what concerns you."

"The crime in the city is getting out of hand."

"Crime is a problem. What do you think we should do about it?"

The man stared at her. "What I think we should do about it? Get the police to stop it; that's their job."

"The police deal with crime after it's happened. They aren't so good at preventing it. Preventing it takes community development. You'll find that it is driven by poverty, isn't that right, Molly?"

Molly straightened as the man glared at her. "Which do you think is most dangerous, drugs or poverty?"

"Drugs, there are too many drugs on the streets." He looked to be moving away.

"Why do you think the drugs are there?" Molly asked

"Because the addicts and junkies want them." The man frowned and edged farther from Molly.

"Right, most of them want drugs because their lives suck. Poverty goes hand in hand with addiction, mental illness, physical illness and more. So maybe the best way to stop the drugs and crime is to eliminate poverty." Molly smiled and tried to look confident.

"We can't do that. It isn't possible. The taxes would sink every good citizen in the country."

"Poverty costs BC somewhere around four billion dollars a year in lost productivity. Not to mention the expenses of maintaining police forces and prisons, the extra healthcare costs." Molly dug out a flyer from her messenger bag and held it out to him.

"You're as crazy as her." The man stomped off, but a woman stopped to ask about daycare and the day went on. A reporter asked if they could take a photo of Agatha talking to someone. No one wanted to until a homeless man picking up trash on the street volunteered.

The photo in the paper wasn't complimentary.

Molly didn't understand why Agatha put herself on the street corners; but it was her campaign, let her run it as she wanted.

Professor Huston had told her politics was a facet of community building and thus, social work. So as well as filling out all the paperwork, she had to write an essay on how work at a thrift shop led to a mayoral campaign.

Between school and the campaign, Molly left early and got home late. Blue was busy on his side too. Brown had his followers handing out pamphlets outside the Loop on Tranquille and the Café on Victoria. They stayed meticulously within the rules, but it worried Molly. Blue's hours were almost as long as hers and he looked tired.

***

**Friday, September 25**

On the opening day of the Café, they had thirty guests come through the door. Blue was thankful no major incidents happened. He knew it would happen sooner rather than later, but having a relatively quiet opening made for good press.

"You were right," said Judy as she looked at the guests talking or playing cards and drinking coffee.

"The kitchen needs more work." Tad, a young man who volunteered in the kitchen at the Loop came out to report to Blue.

There were countless numbers of peanut butter and jam sandwiches handed out

"That's a relief," Blue laughed. "I don't have a good record with being right. I live by my gut."

"Well, you have a smart gut then."

In the following days, the numbers stayed at about thirty people. If they weren't all there at once, they were fine with the Covid restrictions. They had a maximum capacity of twelve guests and four staff. They hadn't found anyone to donate masks in large enough numbers, and the staff had to be scrupulous about getting departing guests to put the masks in the trash. He hated the waste, not just of money but of the masks. But it was the new reality. After four waves, the powers-that-be had stopped predicting this set of health responses would end the pandemic.

Molly dropped in to hand out buttons to the guests. She explained how they could register to vote. The Loop was a mailing address for a large number of people. Blue was astonished at how much mail came for people without home addresses. He set up the same system at the Café.

A young man came in and Molly tensed up. This must be the persistent young man.

"Look, Cam. I'm busy and the answer is going to be no. It will always be no. I have zero interest in getting to know you better." She didn't give him a chance to talk. "Stop following me around and stop asking me to go out."

He reddened. "You would rather hang out with this bunch of junkies?"

"Yes, because they understand the word 'no,'" Molly growled at him. A couple of the men stood up, but Molly waved them back.

Cam grabbed her arm. "You have to listen to me."

"No, Cam, I don't." Molly twisted her arm free and pointed to the door. "Touch me again and I will break your arm. You've been warned."

He hung his head and left.

*This has gone beyond bugging her to harassment.* Blue bit back his words of advice. She wouldn't want him telling her what to do.

***

"Why did you want to meet here this late at night? I want to break it off with Carlotta, so we don't have to sneak around like this?" Cam pleaded.

"Can't a girl be a little kinky?" She reached for his pants, unbuckled his belt, and leaned in close. "I'm not wearing any underwear. Let's celebrate."

Cam dropped his pants and grabbed for her. She laughed and stepped back.

"Don't be a tease." He whined and reached down to pull up his pants. She pushed him over.

"Teasing is just foreplay." She grabbed him with her left hand, and he groaned. At that moment she shoved the knife through his ribs into his heart. "If I leave this in the wound you might survive." She kissed him then pulled the knife free and dropped it. She put the kerchief she'd held it with in her pocket. He grunted and went still. She took the bloody jacket off and laid it over his face.

***

Molly cautiously walked along the back alley. The front door had been locked. The text said to meet Blue in the back, but she'd hoped to walk through the Café.

A dark shape lay on the pavement not moving. *Blue!* She bent down and pushed the thing covering his face aside. In the dim light, the dead eyes of Cameron Robinson stared up at her.

Molly screamed, then the alley was lit by a floodlight. She jumped to her feet.

"I didn't want him to die, just to go away." She wailed.

Molly could see Post call it in before he got out of the car, hand on his holster.

"I tried to stop the bleeding." She fell to her knees and wept.

"Molly Callister. I will have to take you to the station for questioning. Do you understand?"

She nodded her head and stood up. "I know the routine."

Post reminded Molly of her rights anyway, patted her down, handcuffed her, and put her into the car.

Sirens approached and Molly tried to make sense of what had happened. Her hands were covered with blood. Cam was dead, murdered. Her stomach tried to empty, but Molly swallowed and breathed deeply.

They moved her to another car and a different officer drove her to the Battle Street Station and past a garage door. It closed behind them as another constable came through the only other door. She looked bored.

"Booking the perp?"

"Post said she's a material witness." The cop opened the cruiser door and let Molly out. Her legs would barely hold her.

Through the door was a room with a desk piled with paper. The male cop undid her cuffs.

"Photos first." The woman cop pointed to the wall with marks for height on it. "Face the camera. Now left, right." She used a different camera to record the blood stains on Molly's shirt and hands. They made her power-off her phone and empty her pockets into a tray while the woman cop took notes and made Molly sign the list.

"I need your clothes." The cop handed her a set of scrubs. "Put these on." The male cop stepped out into the garage.

Molly took off her shirt, then her jeans as the cop drummed her fingers against her leg.

"Can I wash off the blood?"

"I'll ask." The cop didn't sound like she wanted the bother. She pushed a button on the wall. "Prisoner for the cells."

The door opened with a buzz, and Molly was led to the first cell. The cop pointed into the cell and Molly walked in and let herself drop on the cot. The cell door clanged shut and the cop left her alone.

# Chapter 7

**Monday, September 28**

The phone rang, and Blue snatched it up. It would be Molly apologizing for being so late. She was an adult so had no curfew, but she usually phoned when out late.

"Blue," Molly sounded flat. "I'm in trouble. Come to the police station and bring a lawyer."

"What happened?"

"I can't talk about it on the phone." There was a click, and she was gone.

Blue stared at the phone in his hand. What kind of trouble was she in that needed a lawyer, and more importantly what had happened to make her sound so dead?

*Worry later, act now.*

He called up the only lawyer he knew. They'd helped him and Molly do their wills a year ago. He hadn't seen the point, but she insisted, something to do with one of her courses.

"Conrad, sorry to bother you so late, but I need a lawyer right away."

"I'm guessing criminal? I'll come and if I get out of my depth, I will call in a colleague."

"Meet me at the Battle Street Police Station as soon as you can."

Blue threw a coat on and stopped. He called Judy.

"I need a ride to the police station right now. You're the only person I could think of."

"I'll be right there. It will be a break from paperwork. What's wrong?"

"I don't know."

A few minutes later her car pulled into the parking lot of his building. Blue climbed in and they drove to the police station. Conrad was waiting outside for Blue.

"Thanks, Judy, you have no idea how much I appreciate it."

He ran into the station. A constable came out to meet him.

"The lawyer can go in to talk to Ms. Callister. You'll have to wait."

"Blue…" Conrad said.

"I know, go talk to Molly. I'll be fine out here." *I hope.* The last thing he needed was to give in to a flashback, but Molly needed him.

He perched on a chair and focused on the wanted posters, anything to keep his mind busy.

***

An officer knocked on Molly's cell door "Lawyer's here. I will take you to the interview room."

"All right." Molly pushed herself to her feet and followed the woman to a plain room where the lawyer waited.

"You might not remember me; my name is Conrad." He stood up and waved her to a chair, then took the other chair and pulled a pen and yellow legal pad from his briefcase. "You are safe to talk here. First, tell me if you've been arrested?"

"They detained me for questioning." Molly slumped in the chair.

"Okay, tell me what happened."

"I got a text from Blue to meet him by the Café. When I got there, I saw a body and thought it was Blue. I ran over and tried to stop the bleeding, but he was already dead." She shuddered and stared at her hands, still pink from blood after they let her use a damp towel to wipe them down.

"Who was it? Did you know him?"

"His name is Cam Robinson, he'd been bugging me, not quite harassing me. He's in the same course as me at TRU."

"Do you know why he was bugging you?" Conrad might have been talking over coffee. His calm seeped into Molly, and she breathed deeper.

"I let it slip I had been a hooker in the past. He immediately started asking me out. I said no. Last time I saw him was earlier that day. He grabbed my arm. I told him if he touched me again, I'd break his arm." Molly's face heated. It didn't look good that she'd lost her temper.

"Were there witnesses?"

"A whole room full. It was at the Café."

"Now, I need to hear what you have said to the police." He poised his pen over the pad.

"I don't remember what I said when Constable Post found me. I think it was something about trying to stop the bleeding. I haven't said anything else but asked for a lawyer. I think they had me on suicide watch."

"Are you feeling suicidal?"

"No." A spark of anger flared in Molly's gut. "I didn't kill him."

"Very good." Conrad leaned back. "If they had the evidence, you'd be charged. They can detain you for twenty-four hours before either charging you or letting you go. I expect they'll hang on to you until they've processed the scene and determined if you are the likely killer or just in the wrong place at the wrong time."

"I got a text saying it was from Blue. It had his number and everything. Someone wanted me there."

"Any idea who?"

"None, Cam was the only one with reason to dislike me as far as I know."

"I am going to talk to the police and see if I can get you released, but I can't make any promises."

"Can I see Blue?"

"I'll ask, but probably not until you're released. Wait here and think about what kind of statement you want to give to the police. I'll be back in a few minutes, and we'll go over your statement."

***

Sergeant Ferguson got back to the station as the light was peaking up in the east. At least the Constable hadn't mucked around in the scene, so the evidence was clean enough. He'd canvass the neighbourhood to see if anyone had cameras showing what had happened. Unless something major showed up, it should be a relatively simple case.

Ferguson went to the interview room where the booking sergeant said the suspect was with her lawyer and knocked on the door.

"Come in."

Ferguson set up the video camera and connected it to the computer.

"Let's start with your name ..."

The girl's statement was bare bones: no embellishment, no explanations, no protests that she was innocent. Her lawyer must be pretty good.

"A few questions." Ferguson looked through his notebook. "Did you know the deceased?"

"Only enough to tell him no, I didn't want to date him."

"Why didn't you want to date him?"

"I didn't particularly like him. I didn't really dislike him either." The suspect tightened her lips. Maybe she had disliked him more than she was saying.

"Do you know why he wanted to date you?"

"I don't want to speculate."

"Do you normally carry a knife?"

Molly looked at Conrad who nodded.

"Don't like knives."

"Constable Post stated you were crying 'I only wanted him to go away; I didn't want him dead.'"

"I might have; I thought the body was my father. I don't remember much from seeing the body to Constable Post arriving."

"You know Constable Post?"

"We've had reason to talk." Molly met his gaze.

"Professionally?"

"In his role as a police officer, yes."

"Were you being charged with a crime?"

"Don't answer that." Conrad interrupted.

Ferguson looked at him with annoyance, but they'd run her prints. If she was in the system, they'd find her. "Do you think your lapse of memory would include killing Cameron Robinson?

"I remember finding the body, then panicking. I did not kill Cameron."

"You said you don't like knives. What is your weapon of choice?"

"Don't answer," Conrad said.

"I think I will." The girl met Ferguson's eyes. "Words, Sergeant Ferguson, I use words."

***

Ferguson was confused. Most people were more nervous as the interview progressed, but this one seemed to gain confidence.

She walked back to the cell with her lawyer, escorted by a constable, while Ferguson went out front to talk to her father, the man she called Blue.

"Do you mind answering a few questions?"

"May as well." The man answered. His face was lined and his hand twitched.

"You all right?"

"I don't like police stations."

"They make a lot of people nervous." Ferguson let the silence drag on, but Blue didn't say anything.

"Did you text your daughter this evening?" Ferguson broke the silence, keeping an eye on that twitching hand.

"No." The hand didn't change its rhythm.

"Is your daughter ever a violent person?"

"No." Rhythm still didn't change.

"Is she known to the police?"

"Some of them."

*That's an odd answer.*

"Can you explain that in more detail?"

"She met Constable Post when I was abducted a few years back. She knew Constable Madoc before she was transferred out."

"How did she know Madoc?"

"Through Car 40," Blue said.

"Right, and what was that about?"

"That's Molly's story to tell."

The hand was twitching faster.

"If the police station is that upsetting, why don't you go home? She can call you if she is released."

"I will wait until I know what happened to Molly." Blue crossed his arms.

"Nothing happened to Molly. The question is whether she happened to someone else."

The hand stopped dead and the guy didn't move for so long Ferguson worried he'd had a seizure. He was about to shake the man when he spoke.

"I see, thank you." He turned and walked away to pace the small waiting space.

Ferguson's phone buzzed.

"Ferguson."

"We're finished with the scene for the moment. The body is gone to the coroner. Cause of death is probably a knife to the heart."

"No assumptions." He should know better as a scene of crime officer.

"No, sir."

Ferguson hung up. With any luck, the autopsy wouldn't wait too long. In the meantime, he had work to do.

# Chapter 8

Molly sat in her cell and fought the urge to fall apart. Going to pieces would only make the police more certain that she'd killed Cam.

Maybe if she'd just gone out that one time, he'd be alive. She shuddered. No, that wasn't an option. Somebody murdered him and she happened to stumble on the scene. That didn't make sense. There was the text from Blue. He'd sounded fine when she called.

Was someone setting her up? That couldn't be it. She was just a social work student. Cam was the only one who had an issue with her.

*It had to be a coincidence. It had to be.*

She startled when an officer knocked on her cell door. They came by at odd intervals, probably making sure she didn't kill herself.

"You hungry? I can grab a sandwich from a machine."

"I don't think I could eat." Molly fell over on the bench that served as a bed. *Don't be stupid.* "Wait, maybe I will have something. Thanks."

This wouldn't be over soon; this wasn't like getting picked up for hustling johns. They weren't going to throw her back on the street as too small a fish to bother with.

Conrad said they needed to charge or release her within twenty-four hours. How long had she been here? It had to have been after midnight when she got the text from Blue. She thought it was morning now. At least another sixteen hours before she would know.

The cop came back with the sandwich and a bottle of water, watched her eat, then took the garbage away. She stretched out on the cot.

***

Sergeant Ferguson woke her. "We're kicking you loose, for now. Your clothes are evidence, but you can pick up the rest of your stuff. You can wear the scrubs you have on home. Don't leave town."

Molly ran a hand down the green clothes saying 'Property of the RCMP' across the back. At least they weren't orange. The constable in charge of the cells escorted her to where they'd brought her in, printed and photographed her with all the blood on her. The room made her stomach curdle.

"Here's your stuff. Sign here."

Molly picked up her bag and checked through it. Everything was there.

"Wait, my phone isn't working."

"Maybe the battery's dead. I don't have all day."

Molly pulled out a charger. "Do you have a place to plug this in, just to see if it is the battery?"

The constable sighed but let her plug the phone in. Nothing.

"I know it was working last night."

The constable shoved a form at her. "Fill this out." The thick felt-tipped pen made it a challenge, but Molly finished the form and handed it to the constable. She tossed it in a basket in a way that made Molly sure her complaint wasn't going to be dealt with any time soon.

Molly pushed the phone into her pocket and grabbed her bag. "Thanks, can you show me out to the front. My father will be waiting for me."

The cop walked around the desk. "Follow me."

Blue waited for her in the tiny waiting room.

"Blue!" Molly sat beside him and hugged him. "You've been here all night? Let's get you out of here and into the sun." She pulled him to his feet and guided him out the door. "We're going to take a cab home." One was parked nearby. The driver agreed to take them only after she showed him enough cash for the trip.

Blue followed her up to the apartment like a zombie. The flashbacks must be horrible. Harley welcomed them. Molly sat Blue on the couch, took Harley outside for a minute, and then brought her to lie down beside Blue. She put his hand on the dog's back, then sat on the other side.

***

"Molly?" Blue's voice came out as a rasp. He'd fought flashbacks of fire and blood all night, then sunk into an exhausted stupor.

"We're at home?" Molly slept with her head on his leg. Harley lay with her head on the other leg. Blue shook Molly gently and she sat up.

"Blue, you're awake. I was so worried."

"Sorry to worry you." Blue hugged her tight for a long moment. "You and Harley brought me back."

"I'll make coffee." Molly jumped up and dashed for the kitchen. She came back sooner than he thought possible. "Should be ready in a minute."

She sat beside Blue until the coffee stopped gurgling, then fetched them cups.

"You all right to talk about it?" Blue cupped his hands around the warm mug.

"You all right to listen?" Molly blew on her coffee but didn't take a sip.

"Yes."

"Okay then," Molly sat in silence, then took a long breath. "I was late at the shop. There were last-minute changes to a flyer, and I had to make sure they copied properly. Our office isn't state of the art. Just as I was leaving, I got a text from you saying you needed my help with something at the Café."

"I didn't send a text," Blue said.

"It came from your number and everything. It read like one of your texts. I walked from the shop to the Café and went around the back like your text said."

"Would I ask you to walk through a back alley late at night?"

"I tried the front door, but there was no answer."

"Then you went to the back…"

"I saw a body and thought it was you." She let out a sob. "I hadn't hurried and thought you'd been killed waiting for me."

"Who was it?"

"Cameron Robinson, the guy who came to the Café earlier in the day. He's been bugging me constantly to go out with him."

"And you gave him the heave-ho. Why would he come back?"

"I don't know, maybe he got a text like me." Molly rubbed her temples.

"Go on."

"There isn't much left. Constable Post showed up and I was detained."

"Did Conrad get to you?"

"Yeah, he was great. But the interview didn't take very long, not like in the movies. I spent most of the day sleeping in the cell."

"They're still looking for evidence. Likely they'll be keeping an eye on you. Killers do stupid things like brag about their crime."

"I'm not stupid enough to commit the crime."

"Point taken. Did you touch anything at the scene but the body?"

"No, I was crying and trying to stop the bleeding, but I think he was already dead when I got there." Molly shivered. "Oh wait, I moved whatever covered his face. That's when I recognized Cam."

"No knife or anything?"

"Didn't see any."

"Must have been horrible."

"And sitting all day in the police station waiting room wasn't horrible for you?" Molly sipped at her coffee. "I thought you were dead for the second time in two days."

"Pride and worry are a dangerous combination. I should have trusted Conrad to do his job."

"So now what?" Molly looked at him with a combination of fear and trust in her eyes.

"You live your life. Nothing else to do unless you plan to hole up in the apartment for the foreseeable future. Don't talk about what happened. Let the police do their thing. Despite the movies, they are usually competent."

***

## Saturday, October 1

"Ferguson." He answered his phone.

"We have a problem with the fingerprints on the knife." The crime scene supervisor sounded annoyed rather than worried.

"Well?" Ferguson tapped his foot impatiently.

"There aren't any prints. It looks like the killer wore gloves, or a glove anyway, or used something else to keep their prints off the handle of the knife. There is a partial etched into the blade, like someone didn't wipe off a fingerprint, but it could be years old. It is unlikely to be good enough to match to the suspect's prints."

"No glove or anything like one came in the evidence. Good work." Ferguson cut off the call and phoned the people still monitoring the crime scene. "Look for gloves, or a glove, or something that could be wrapped around a knife handle to keep prints from the knife."

"Why would she wear gloves, then take them off after she killed him?"

"Don't worry about why, just look for them."

One thing he'd learned over the years was that criminals did absurd things.

*Maybe it's time to have another conversation with Ms. Callister.* He let dispatch know to watch for her and report. He'd go pick her up himself in an unmarked car, no need to give the crazies a head start.

He headed to meet the coroner for the autopsy.

Ferguson had lost count of the autopsies he'd attended. They all had the antiseptic smell of a hospital mixed with death.

"Autopsy of Cameron Robinson, aged 21. In generally good health…" The coroner droned on for the video. "…hmm, that's odd."

"What have you got?" Ferguson peered at where the coroner was poking about the knife wound.

"No hesitation marks, one blow, between the ribs. To strike the left ventricle, I'm guessing, but we'll know when we open him up. Most people will take a couple of times to stab that deeply.

"That is strange," Ferguson said but reserved any speculation until the end of the autopsy.

"Right…" She went back to describing the body.

When she cut open the chest cavity, she confirmed the strike to the heart. "If she'd left the knife in, the poor kid might have made it. I'd give him a one in ten chance."

They went through the rest of the autopsy without finding any other oddities.

"Thanks, Doc." Ferguson took the gown and the rest of the PPE off, then washed his hands before heading outside to breathe fresh air.

# Chapter 9

**Sunday, October 3**

Getting ready for the All-Candidates Meeting was a bigger deal than Molly expected. They had to print more leaflets. Make more buttons with the ancient button maker Agatha unearthed from the back of the shop. Ask a couple of people to ask questions to get the discussion going.

Agatha gave Molly a folder full of papers with sticky notes and highlighting.

"They won't expect much from an old woman like me, but I plan to surprise them. I've been doing my research." Molly's stomach sank. Was Agatha planning to quote obscure anarchist leaders again? She sat down in a corner and carefully read through the papers. They ranged from discussion of high-density infill construction in the downtown core to create more property tax income to measures to end homelessness through 'Housing First.' Research on how a safe supply of drugs lowers the number of overdoses and death attributable to opioids. The list was mind-boggling.

Agatha came over to where Molly sat on an old rocking chair with a piece of plywood screwed onto the seat. "I'll wave you over if I do, put yourself in the crowd where I can see you and pay attention to how the people around you are reacting.

"I can do that. I think a lot of students from Thompson Rivers University will be there."

Molly went back to reading until she was called upon to coddle the old photocopier into working. None of the other students had continued to help, preferring to spend spare time over coffee or beer.

***

Blue looked out the window at the protest. They'd started the day after Cameron Robinson's death, blaming the Café because it had happened nearby in the alley. The Café had closed at five and the murder had happened around midnight, but that didn't matter. The group chanted "Justice for Cameron" and "Close the murder café." Fortunately, the windows muddied the noise.

The number of people in the Café dropped drastically as the guests didn't want to walk past the protesters. They'd started blocking the back entrance. Bylaws warned them off, but still, one leaned against the wall, glaring at anyone going in or out of the building.

Blue had suggested Lee stop coming over until the fuss died down. The agency agreed with him, and that left him to suffer through the days with the one or two staff who showed up and braved the picket line.

The All-Candidates Meeting up by TRU was tomorrow, and he'd promised to be there and bring some guests if possible.

He worried about Molly, who hadn't mentioned the murder or her almost-arrest since the evening they'd got home from the police station. He didn't talk about the protest being specifically about the murder, but the press was having a field day. That John Brown, a mayoral candidate was one of the principal organizers only made the story juicier.

Blue hoped the campaign would take John Brown away from the protests at the Café, but the man apparently was basing his entire campaign on them. One of the other candidates showed up for an hour yesterday while the news cameras rolled. They interviewed him, then left without talking to John Brown.

Paperwork waited for him on his desk, so he worked on scheduling and payroll while keeping one eye on the guests. A constable walked through the protest which parted like the sea around Moses. The chant faded until he'd gone in the front door, paying them not the slightest bit of attention.

"I'm canvassing the neighbourhood." The constable said. "Did you see this man around on the 27th of September or before?" He held up a photo.

"He was in that afternoon, asking my daughter out for a date. She said no. He didn't take it well, and she showed him out the door.

"Where did they know each other from?"

"They're both social work students at TRU. This wasn't the first time he'd tried to get her to go out with him."

"Do you know why?"

"I wouldn't want to speculate." Blue kept his gaze even. The cop went and showed the picture to the few guests who were present. Most of them shook their head without saying anything, but one older guy who was pushing the limit of the no-intoxication rule regaled the officer with the whole story. He embellished it, making the two-second altercation into a full-blown fight.

"She said if she ever saw him again, she'd kill him."

Erica tried to do damage control, but the officer wasn't buying it. He was clearly delighted with his discovery and hustled back to his car and drove off. Blue grabbed his phone to give Molly a heads up, but an argument broke out between the storyteller and another guest. Blue eventually had to ask both to leave. They had been shouting loudly, and Blue hoped the protesters were too busy with their chant to listen. But the way John Brown was glaring triumphantly through the window suggested that he, at least, had heard the row.

The guests left after that, and they closed the Café early. Blue wrote up an incident report about the argument and added it to the mountain of statistics, reports and input from guests that threatened to swamp his desk.

He thought about going to the thrift shop to talk to Molly but worried it would look like he was colluding with her if he was there when the police showed up. He didn't think they would overlook the story of the fight and would probably bring her in for questioning again. His hand twitched toward his phone, but he sighed and went back to his paperwork. Maybe it would be better if she didn't know, and her surprise was genuine.

When he finally made it home, Blue was surprised to see Molly in the kitchen cooking supper.

"I'd thought you'd be at the shop late tonight. Something came up at the Café today," and Blue filled her in on the 'witness' and near fight.

"Agatha sent us all home early. The meeting is at four tomorrow, and she wants everyone rested. Nothing I can do about the story now." She set plates and cutlery on the table and put the casserole on a trivet. "Food's up."

They sat and dug in. As usual, Blue was struck by the difference between her cooking and his. He cooked food to eat, while she cooked food to enjoy.

"Are you sure you should still be working the campaign? You have a lot on your plate."

"Is this about how you don't want poverty to be a campaign issue?" Molly put her fork down and glared at him.

"No, this is about you backing off a bit given the cops have a target on your back."

"I'm not allowed to 'back off.'" Molly leaned back and crossed her arms. "This is one of my courses, and even if it wasn't, I wouldn't leave Agatha in the lurch.

"How is Agatha doing? I saw in the paper she's dead last in the latest poll." Blue made a peace offering.

Molly relaxed. "She doesn't believe in polls, but she plans to finish the second half of the campaign strong. Believe it or not, she's been studying the platforms of the other candidates and is looking to refute them or steal their thunder."

"Sounds like she'd be a good mayor."

"Probably, but she doesn't have the existing backing that the councillors have. People know their faces and what stands they've taken in the past. Maybe we should have gone for city councillor instead."

"How's your work going?"

"I am gaining an understanding of why you hate paperwork so much."

Blue laughed. "They should have a course just on doing paperwork. The funders want so much information about everything."

"I got a taste of it in statistics, but this is a whole new level. If a volunteer brings a thermos of coffee into the shop, that isn't a donation. If the coffee shop sends over a bunch of coffee, that is a donation and needs to be recorded as a donation and expense. Most of the donations are under fifty dollars and made anonymously, but a few need to be receipted and recorded. Since we're using the thrift shop as a headquarters, it has to be expensed. It is easier to be the candidate than the financial officer."

"Okay, enough shop talk. Let's take Harley for a walk then watch a movie."

"That sounds good. I get to choose the movie."

# Chapter 10

## Monday, October 4

Ferguson stared at the note in a clear plastic bag.

It read. *Molly, print another 100 of leaflet 2.*

"She never mentioned the jacket. Didn't mention a fight with the deceased either. At least we have an idea where she will be."

"What are you thinking?" Sergeant Hassim said

"Who's printing a pile of leaflets these days?" He glanced at his partner.

"She's working on a campaign." Sergeant Hassim grinned. "And the All-Candidates Meeting is at the university."

"We keep this low-key for now." Ferguson looked at his watch. "The All-Candidates' Meeting should be well underway. I'll pick her up. You review the last interview. We'll crack this one yet."

***

The university auditorium was crowded for the times of Covid. People wore masks from the standard clinical blue to wildly coloured to faces with clown mouths or fangs. The air buzzed with conversation.

Molly handed out leaflets. Some people walked past without looking at her; others took the paper and peered at the information on the way to their seats. One of the ladies who was a regular at the shop stood at the other door. She thought she spotted Carolyn in the crowd, but someone wanting a leaflet distracted her.

The stage was set up for the candidates with bottles of water on the seats. and the regulation two-metre space between their chairs. The mayoral candidates would speak first, then the councillors. Open questions would follow.

Though she wasn't speaking, Molly fought butterflies in her stomach. She had Agatha's notes in her messenger bag slung over her shoulder. The remaining space was full of leaflets, but she was running low.

The candidates came out to polite applause from the audience.

"Welcome to the TRU All-Candidates Meeting." A rep from the student council was moderating the meeting. He introduced the candidates in alphabetical order. By the meagre applause she received, Molly figured Agatha was running in last place, but Agatha smiled as if she'd got a standing ovation.

"The candidates for mayor drew lots to determine the speaking order. Our first speaker has been a councillor for three terms…"

The councillor's speech was carefully structured not to point fingers at the previous administration while suggesting that as mayor he would do better. The next candidate followed the same pattern, but she suggested that property taxes needed to be lowered and incentives to build created to encourage more new housing.

Then it was John Brown's turn. "Kamloops has become a hotbed of crime. One of the most dangerous cities in the country to live in. The reason is we are too easy on criminals and vagrants. A so-called café was opened downtown on Victoria. These are the same people who opened the Loop on Tranquille and caused the crime rate to go up. There has already been a murder and it hasn't been open a month yet. We need to stop coddling these people and let them know, they obey the law or get locked up. If they don't like it, they're free to move on to the next city. We'll even pay for a bus ticket."

He ranted for the rest of his allotted time and didn't stop until the sound people cut the power to his microphone.

Next up was Agatha. "I've been spending my time on the streets listening to you. All of you. Crime is an issue as Mr. Brown pointed out so vigorously. Housing is an issue, as is the paradox that workers are staying away from some jobs and overloading the application systems of other positions."

People in the crowd were nodding their heads.

"I want to point out that crime in Kamloops has been steadily worsening, but it is doing so in direct proportion to the amount of heavy-handed 'tough on crime' policies put in place. Almost as if more police, more security, more bylaw officers are working to increase crime rates. Perhaps it is time to consider a different tack."

Agatha waited for the murmuring to die down. Some of the crowd were nodding slowly while others shook theirs vigorously.

"Businesses are suffering from a double blow. Employment costs are going up, but revenue isn't following suit. The problem may be that there just isn't enough money for people to spend, or it could be consumers are cautious after years of fighting a pandemic, record fires and floods. We need to find some way of putting money in the pockets of the citizens of Kamloops. Tax breaks are great, but only for those people who are fortunate enough to pay taxes.

She took a long breath.

"Housing continues to be not only scarce but expensive.  Someone working a forty-hour week at fifteen dollars an hour will be using at least half their salary just to pay the rent or mortgage on their home.

"Fortunately, there is a possible solution to all these problems. Sadly, a universal basic income is not in the municipal jurisdiction, but we could, as other cities do, lobby for one. What is within our reach is using zoning and breaks on building permits to make sure that every new development - whether rental, condo, or detached housing - includes housing for people on the lower end of the income scale." Agatha caught Molly's eyes and smiled.

"Many cities have used the principles of 'housing first' to reduce the homelessness, and coincidentally reduce crime. Not, I hasten to add, because homelessness is the root of criminal behaviour, but because poverty is directly related to homelessness, to crime, to lack of money to spend at our local businesses—"

"Ms. Callister." Molly turned to see Sergeant Ferguson standing at her elbow. "I'm going to have to ask you to come with me. We have a few more questions for you."

"Can I stay to hear the end of Agatha's speech?"

"Sorry, but I don't have the luxury of spending time listening to politics." He looked relaxed, but Molly expected that could change at a moment's notice.

"Okay, let's go and get this over with." Molly walked out of the auditorium with Sergeant Ferguson at her side. At least he wasn't in uniform.

Agatha stumbled in her speech, then recovered.

***

They pulled into the back of the station, and Molly followed the Sergeant to a different interview room. This one had a glass section where she supposed others could stand and watch the proceedings. She was directed to sit in a chair facing the glass and left alone.

The first thing she'd said was that she wanted her lawyer.

A woman she didn't recognize brought in a phone.

"Am I under arrest?" Molly's pulse pounded in her ears.

"Not yet. Tap on the door when you're done." The woman left as Molly dug out Conrad's card and turned her back to the glass wall.

"Molly Callister for Conrad." She said when the receptionist answered the phone.

"Sorry, he's in court. Do you want to leave a message?" the receptionist responded

"I've been picked up for questioning, again. They seem more determined this time."

"You can ask them to wait for Conrad to attend, or I can send an associate."

"I'll wait for Conrad. How long is he likely to be?"

"I will send him a text, but at least a couple of hours."

"Thank you."

Molly hung up and leaned back. She didn't want to wait hours in this room, but even less did she want to talk to the police without a lawyer at her side. She got up and rapped on the door.

The woman came in again and took the phone.

"My lawyer is in court. He should be here in a couple hours," Molly said.

"You think we have time to just sit around waiting?" The female officer, whose name tag read 'Sergeant Hassim,' frowned

"I'm sure you have some paperwork to do. I know I do." Molly wished she hadn't needed to let them take her messenger bag while she was in interrogation.

"You've got me there."

The woman left Molly with her thoughts.

***

Conrad arrived three hours later.

"Have they said anything more than they have more questions?"

"No."

"Let's go over everything again to see if something comes up." Conrad grilled her for an hour before he was satisfied that he was up to date on everything.

"We may as well let them know we're ready." Conrad knocked on the door. "Ready when you are."

"I'll let them know," the constable replied.

Molly half expected to wait another few hours, but Sergeant Ferguson and Sergeant Hassim showed up almost immediately. Ferguson carried a brown file box. He turned on the video camera.

"For the record, I am Sergeant Ferguson."

"Sergeant Hassim," the woman said.

"We are interviewing Molly Callister in the presence of her lawyer."

After the formalities, Sergeant Hassim pulled a piece of paper in a plastic sleeve from the box and placed it on the table. "Recognize this?"

"It's a note Agatha wrote me." Molly wrinkled her forehead. "Why do you have it?"

"Let us ask the questions, Ms. Callister," Ferguson said. "So you definitely identify this as a note that belongs to you."

"Yes." Molly bit back the questions she wanted to ask.

"In your statement, you failed to mention you fought with the deceased earlier the day of the murder," Sergeant Hassim interjected.

"He asked me out, I said no. He grabbed my arm. I broke his grip then frog-marched him out the door."

Sergeant Hassim looked at her notes. "Telling him if you saw him again, you'd kill him."

"Telling him if he touched me again without permission, I'd break his arm," Molly corrected her.

Conrad shook his head but didn't say anything.

"That isn't what our witness said." Sergeant Ferguson leaned forward.

"Witness. Singular." Conrad shook his head. "There were at least a dozen people present when Robinson grabbed my client's arm, which is assault. I expect you didn't find a second witness to corroborate that fairy tale."

Ferguson frowned and Conrad made a calm down gesture with his hand.

Hassim picked another plastic bag out of the box.

"Recognize this?"

Molly stared at the bloody jacket, she could hardly make out its original colour— her breath caught, and she flipped the jacket over. *Shit.*

"It is my jacket. It was stolen a day or two before the murder."

"Did you report it?" Hassim asked.

"It is a thrift shop jacket, hardly worth a police report," Molly snapped back.

"Convenient," Ferguson interjected.

"Yes." Molly's stomach turned to ice. "Someone wore my jacket to kill Robinson and left it there for you to find. That stretches the bounds of coincidence."

Conrad winced and shook his head at her.

"My thought exactly," Ferguson growled and leaned farther forward.

"Is there blood on the inside of the jacket?" Molly fired the question at Hassim.

"Yes," Hassim said and turned red.

"We ask the questions." Ferguson stood to loom over her.

"Then I won't ask a question." Molly refused to back down, ignoring the cutting motion Conrad made. "You haven't matched the blood pattern from the inside of the jacket to my shirt, or you'd be throwing that in my face."

"Ms. Callister…"

"Back off, Ferguson," Conrad said calmly. "Bullying your witness will only get the testimony challenged in court. If you don't have any more questions, we'll be on our way."

"Don't leave town." Ferguson turned and walked out of the room.

"I'll show you out." Hassim stood and led them to the processing room where Molly exchanged her receipt for her bag.

"Blast," she said. "I was going to ask about my phone. It turned into a brick while they had it in the locker. The guy at the cellphone repair place couldn't do anything. Said the battery overheated and fried the phone."

"Interesting," Conrad said. "I know a guy. Want to leave it with me?"

"Sure." Molly dug it out of the bag. "Don't know why I'm carrying around a dead phone."

"You played a dangerous game with Ferguson. Make him angry enough and he'll see it as a contest between him and you and not look for other suspects."

"Somebody set me up." Molly clenched her fists.

"It is beginning to look that way."

"I'm going to start paying more attention to who is nearby."

"No playing detective. That doesn't work out so well in real life." Conrad frowned at her.

"Right, just watching my back," Molly said.

"Do you need a ride home?"

A picture of the bloody jacket ran through Molly's mind, and she shivered. "I do, thanks."

# Chapter 11
## Tuesday, October 5

"Where did you vanish to?" Blue rubbed Harley's ears, but his attention was on Molly.

"Ferguson picked me up again for questioning. The jacket found at the scene was mine. It was stolen a few days before the murder. My phone went AWOL for most of a day too. I thought it was just that I couldn't find it in my bag, but it bricked while I was in custody the first time."

"Bricked?"

"Dead, wouldn't charge, wouldn't start up. Might as well have been a brick."

"Did you tell Sergeant Ferguson?"

"I filled out a complaint form, but no, I didn't mention it to Ferguson."

"Sergeant Ferguson." Blue sighed. "If you practice respect, you can always be deliberately rude when you want, but you can't take back rude out of habit."

"That makes sense, but it isn't easy."

"Aside from the jacket, what did he want?"

"He got some wild tale from the Café about the argument with Cam. Made it sound like something out of an action movie."

"The others didn't want to talk to the police about you," Blue explained.

"That's fine, I get it, but that leaves the wild tale as the only one."

"I'll mention to them that if they are asked again, to tell the truth."

"No more fantasies, just what happened."

"I will see to it."

"Now I need to get to Agatha and apologize for bailing on her." Molly stood and stretched. "Thanks, Blue."

She left the apartment. Blue wanted to hold onto her and keep her safe, but she'd grown into a confident woman. All he'd do was smother her.

***

"That woman, she made a fool of me." John Brown paced in the cramped office he'd rented for the election.

"Sorry, Papa, I never saw her being that smart. She seemed so ditsy." Carolyn dropped her eyes.

"Now, how am I going to fix this hell hole of a city?"

"Something to discredit her?" She looked up at him.

"It has to be the truth, or the media will tear me apart." He smacked a fist into his palm.

"Molly, the girl who helps that woman, she left partway through her boss's speech."

"I saw that. Young people are so rude. You said she is a whore. Maybe she picked up someone."

"Better than that," Carolyn leaned forward in her chair. "That was a plainclothes policeman, I'm certain. What would the police want with her?"

John Brown stopped pacing and furrowed his brow.

"She'd committed a crime? If that woman has a whore on her team, who knows what else is going on? But we need proof, not *maybes*. And that doesn't explain a plainclothes officer arresting her like that. She has to have done something major."

"Most criminals can't stop at one crime." Carolyn smiled wider. "What if she was involved in that murder? I saw her arguing with the victim more than once."

"He looked like such a nice young man, and everyone had only good things to say about him on the funeral home's website. How awful for his family to lose such a son."

"It wouldn't hurt to ask what the police wanted with her, would it?" Carolyn looked at her feet.

"You are a good daughter; I thank God for bringing you into my life."

"As do I, Papa, as do I."

***

Guilt stabbed at Molly as Agatha put a hand to her mouth. "That's horrible," Agatha whispered. They were drinking weak tea in the back of the thrift shop.

"I should have told you about my past right away."

"Nonsense." Agatha hugged her. "You saved me from withering away in despair. I don't care what background you come from."

"But now the police are questioning me. What if that is leaked to the press?"

"Innocent until proven guilty is a foundational principle of our justice system. I will not throw you to the wolves."

"Okay, if you say so." Molly couldn't help but wonder if she should quit anyway, but that would be letting Agatha down.

The phone rang and Agatha answered. The conversation was short and one-sided. When Agatha hung up, she was pale.

"The owner is angry that I've been running my campaign out of the thrift shop. She wants me out today, and the men are coming tomorrow to clear it out. The only reason she isn't taking me to court is I don't have any money." She wiped tears from her cheeks, then breathed deeply.

Molly unclenched her fists and forced her voice to be even. "Let's take what we can and get out of here."

"The only thing that matters is Dale; the rest is junk." Agatha jumped up and went into the back room and came out with a small blanket and a rolling suitcase.

Molly found a box and put the printed leaflets in it along with the last of the buttons. After the professional polished ones the other candidates had, they looked childish. Molly shook her head and looked around for anything else they might need, then added a pad of paper and a couple pens to the box

Agatha picked up Dale and wrapped him in the blanket. Dale complained bitterly but snuggled into Agatha's arms when she stroked his fur.

Molly led Agatha to the Café. It was raining, and she wished she'd got a plastic bag or something to protect the box. At the Café, the protesters had melted in the rain.

The small crowd inside welcomed her like a celebrity, crowding around her.

"You were in that picture with Bill in the paper."

"You running for mayor?"

"I'll vote for you."

"Now, now, let her sit and drink some coffee." Erica put a cup and a plate with a peanut butter sandwich in front of Agatha. Agatha sat with a sigh and put Dale on the floor. The other guest sat as close as they were allowed by the social distancing rules

"Molly, maybe you can tell me what's going on?" Erica scanned the crowd with a frown.

"Agatha got evicted from the thrift shop where she was living. They've been calling her the homeless candidate, but now that's true."

"Agatha can leave her stuff with me," Erica said immediately.

"I can't impose on you, Erica." Agatha put her cup down as Dale jumped up on the table.

"You helped me; now I'm helping you. It isn't imposing. I would take you in if it wouldn't get me evicted." Erica put her hand out to pet Dale.

He hissed at her. "Where did you pick up this big softie?"

"I sort of inherited him. A friend wanted me to take care of him when she was gone."

"Got it, so what do you need for a campaign office?" Erica asked.

"I don't know; maybe I should back out." Agatha poked at the sandwich and sighed.

"Not a chance," Molly said. "We need an office that can be dedicated specifically to the campaign. We should really pay rent on it. I was counting the rent for the thrift shop against the office."

"I got a shed in the backyard I don't use. Can't say the shed is warm and dry. You could use that as your official office like and work out of here." Erica put a hand on Agatha's shoulder.

"What would Blue say to that?" Agatha asked.

"What would Blue say to what?" Blue came in from the kitchen.

"I just said Agatha could do her mayor stuff from here. She needs a warm place to work."

"Why not? Just be aware that John Brown and his cronies protest here every day."

"He doesn't scare me," Agatha said, "and he can't stop me from coming here."

"True enough. Maybe he'll stay away since you handed him his ass on a plate at the All-Candidate's Meeting." Blue grinned. "That was quite the speech."

"I wish I'd been there to see the rest of it." Molly looked down.

"Wasn't your fault, dear." Agatha patted Dale and put the cup in front of him to lap up some coffee.

"Does he like beer too?" Erica asked.

"Wouldn't know; I've been sober since I got him."

"Good for you." Erica hugged Agatha. "I have two years sober next month."

"The next debate is on the fourteenth," Agatha rubbed her hands, the gloom evaporating from her. "I'm looking forward to seeing how the other candidates' policies shift. We're in the home stretch. I'll walk the streets more and hear what people are thinking.

"I'll talk to the students at TRU and get an idea of how they took the debate." Molly paced about. "I'd like to think some of the population of TRU are forward thinkers."

A crash and the sound of broken glass came from the kitchen. Blue dashed through to the back door to try to catch a glimpse of who threw it.

Guests looked around fearfully, and some of them left through the front door.

Molly went into the kitchen to check out the mess and picked her way through the broken glass. It was wrapped in crumpled paper held on with an elastic. She pulled it off and went back to the main room.

"This was wrapped around the rock they tossed through the window." Molly dropped it on the table.

*We know Molly Callister is a prostitute and a criminal. Withdraw or we'll go to the press.*

"They think this will scare me off?" Molly wanted to scream, to overturn tables and kick the chairs. "They've just made me angry."

"Calm down, Molly." Agatha raised her hands. "Maybe we should back off."

"Molly's right." Blue reached for the paper and then drew his hand back. "If we let this slide, it will only get worse. Who will the next rock be aimed at?"

"Either we try to deny it, which will just make us liars," Molly ground the words out through a clenched jaw, "or we beat them to the punch. Blue, do you have that contact at the CBC radio? I'll give them an exclusive story."

"That may be going a bit too far." Blue met Molly's eyes, but she didn't look away.

"It is a part of me like the needle tracks. I faced it and won. I'm not running away now. I need to face this. Nobody who matters will care."

"Okay." Blue pulled out his phone. "Hi, I have a story for you…now. We could always take it to CFAR. That's right…it has to do with a rock through the window of a candidate's office. Do you want to come here, or we come there…we'll be right over."

"It's set. Let's go." Blue grabbed his jacket. "Might as well walk over. Erica, get someone to put wood over that window."

"Are you sure about this?" Agatha took Molly's hands and squeezed them, then let them go.

"Yes." Molly put the paper in her pocket.

"Then I'm coming too. I want them to know I'm proud of my financial officer."

Molly started having second thoughts on the short walk to the CBC studio, but she pushed them away.

The producer met them at the door. "This is very unusual. We'll put you in a booth with one of our reporters and see what comes out. Then decide whether to run it."

"That's fine," Molly said. "This is why we're here.

She handed the scrawled note to the producer. "There are a dozen witnesses who heard the glass break."

"I see." Her mouth thinned. "This way." She led them into a foyer one door led back to offices another into a booth with a glass window. "James here will do the interview."

Inside the sound booth felt strange, like the air pressure was different.

"I'm here with Molly Callister. Molly, tell us what happened." The reporter smiled at her.

"I was at a planning session with Agatha Howard; I'm her financial officer. This note came through a window wrapped around a rock." She read the note aloud and handed it to the producer. "I'm here to clear up a few things. First, I *was* a prostitute, a drug addict, and a criminal. I'm not anymore."

"And you are stating this …"

"Because I won't be blackmailed."

"How long ago was this?" James tilted his head.

"Five years ago, then I met Blue, and he helped me get off the street. I went to something like rehab for a year, and now I'm in my fourth year of Social Work at TRU."

"You aren't afraid that the revelation about your past will affect your schooling?

"They already know. I applied from a program for getting girls off the street. They only cared about my marks and references." Molly took a breath. She'd worked hard for those marks.

"You must have been rather young when you started, uh, selling your services..."

"I started at thirteen, turning tricks for the boys at school; it wasn't a big leap from that to the street. I think I was twenty-one when I met Blue."

"What was it like as a prostitute?"

"Imagine being sexually assaulted every day and having to pretend you enjoyed it. I needed the drugs to survive. I stole from the johns when I had a chance." Molly scrubbed her eyes and blinked away tears. "I'm not proud of my past, but I am proud that I've come through my past and survived. I have my scars, but they're proof I'm alive."

"So why talk about it now?"

"I revealed my past to a class this fall, most of whom were very supportive. It isn't something I spend any time bragging about, but I don't hide it. Now someone is trying to blackmail my employer through my past. I'm showing them I will not be shamed back into some corner." Molly met James' eyes.

"How do you think the constituents will respond?" He asked.

"I hope they will see me as a woman who has fought out of a very dark place and plans to help others win the same battle. If they choose to pity me or despise me, that's their loss." She leaned back and crossed her arms to hide the shaking.

"How will your boss react?"

"Agatha's out there waiting to add her support." Molly pointed to the lobby. "I've told her my story, and it only made us closer."

"Agatha Howard isn't your usual mayoral candidate." James grinned.

"She could be the best thing to happen to Kamloops this decade. We'll see what the voters think."

"Any last words of advice for anyone listening?"

"Everyone has dark secrets they don't want told, but it is possible to live through them and rise above them. Ask for as much help as you need and surround yourself with people who love you, not who you were or weren't in the past."

"That was Molly Callister, responding to a blackmail attempt."

"We'll get a few words from Agatha Howard to round out the interview, then we can run it on the local news.

"Thank you."

"You're going to be a hell of a social worker."

Molly left the booth, and Agatha went in to answer a few questions. She came out teary-eyed ten minutes later and hugged Molly.

"Let's go next door and grab a coffee," Blue said. "I, for one, am in desperate need."

***

"You can crash on our couch." Molly shivered in the cold wind.

"I'll be fine." Agatha didn't look cold, but her hands were buried deep in her coat pockets. "It isn't the first time I've been kicked out onto the street. I can stay at the shelter for the night, Erica has Dale and anything else that really matters to me. You hang onto my notes for me."

Molly wanted to argue, but the older woman met her gaze evenly, almost daring her to protest.

Agatha reminded Molly of her friends the Pointed Shoes ladies. Agatha had had a rough life, but not the good fortune which made the Pointed Shoes both comfortable and radical.

# Chapter 12
## Wednesday, October 6

"Does she have no shame?" John Brown stomped around his office. "She just announced to the world she is a harlot. I can't believe I trail her in the polls.

"She used to be one in the past." Carolyn pouted. "But no one will listen to you about something in her past now. We need something in the present."

"So, what's your advice? Spit it out, girl." He immediately regretted taking his spleen out on the girl, but he never apologized except to God.

"We haven't learned why the police wanted to talk to her. The past is the past, but something in the present involving her with the police - that would be a completely different thing."

"Even if we were to find out, how would we use it? The police aren't going to spill their secrets to be spread about the city."

"All we need is a hint. I know a journalist who will take the bait." Carolyn pulled a photo from her purse. "I took a picture of the police officer and Callister. He's Sergeant Ferguson of Major Crimes. Why would an ex-prostitute be of interest to major crimes?"

"Why indeed?" John Brown stopped his pacing. "Maybe she lied about being an ex-whore. I'm sure once a whore, always a whore."

Carolyn blushed red. "That's such a … crude word." She took a deep breath. "I don't think being a … whore is a major crime."

"Maybe she's covering it up. Didn't you say that young man who was murdered knew what she was? Maybe he knew she was still working her trade."

"And she killed him to keep it quiet?" Carolyn sounded doubtful.

"Remember, she is nothing like you. She'd commit any crime if she was threatened."

"I will show the picture to my journalist friend. Maybe we can stir something up."

***

"That little minx." Sergeant Ferguson grinned malevolently. "Why would she admit to being a hooker in the past, if not to hide something in the present?"

"I'm not sure I follow." Hassim shifted at her desk. "From the sound of it, she was being blackmailed."

"If she was being blackmailed, why didn't she come to us?"

"Would you in her situation?" Hassim said. "We've backed her into a corner. She isn't likely to trust us with anything."

"Don't tell me you sympathize with the girl?" Ferguson raised an eyebrow. His phone rang and he held up a hand. "Ferguson here."

"This is Brad Thoms with 'Wake Up Kamloops.' Sergeant Ferguson, would you comment on the reason you took Molly Callister into custody on the night of the All-Candidates Meeting?"

"What?"

"Come on, I have a photo of you standing by her elbow, and she doesn't look happy. Is she involved in the death of Cameron Robinson?"

"Where did you hear that?"

"What other crime would she be involved in? The murder happened outside the Café her adopted father runs. Maybe Robinson was trying to put the squeeze on her? I heard he had an unhealthy fixation on her."

"I can't comment on that."

"He asked her out several times and tried to grab her, and she tossed him hard."

"I heard about that, in the Café, but there is some doubt—"

"Not in the Café, on the Peterson Trail, and his buddies watched. They had to restrain him from attacking her."

"Not the other way?"

"Not according to my sources."

"I can't confirm or deny she's a person of interest in any investigation." Ferguson snapped into the phone and hung up. "Let's see how she wiggles out of that. It's time to play hardball."

"Aren't you supposed to run something like that past the Inspector?"

Ferguson smirked. "I'd better go and beg forgiveness before the shit hits the fan."

***

Bradley Thoms put his phone in his pocket. The cop had all but told him in plain language that Callister was being investigated for murder. He sat at the computer and typed out a quick story. Nothing definite that could get his ass sued, but enough innuendo for the dimmest reader to read between the lines. Before he hit post, he searched her name, and what came up made him grin broadly. He quickly added information to his story and posted it on his blog.

Molly Callister has a history beyond being a simple prostitute. She was involved in what was described as a gang war which ended with an explosion on the North Shore near MacDonald Park. She was treated for unspecified injuries. A year later her adoptive father, Blue, was allegedly abducted and was certainly a witness to another gang-style shoot-out. Now she is being investigated by the police. A source suggested she might be a person of interest in the murder of Cameron Robinson in the alley behind the Café that Blue manages. It is all a little too much to be a coincidence. This reporter wonders if her gang days are really so far behind her.

He had ten thousand followers, but if he was lucky, this could go viral and put him into the big time. His fingers flew across the keyboard.

Rumour has it that Molly Callister, who claims to be being coerced by an unknown person or persons, has a more colourful past than she described. She was rescued from a building destroyed by a powder explosion that rocked the North Shore. She and an unnamed girl were allegedly about to be sold to a gang in Vancouver. Blue, whom she considers her father, was also rescued and treated for gunshots.

The next year, he was abducted following a suspicious fire in his building. The insurance company refused to pay, citing evidence of arson. Unconfirmed rumours suggested he was seen in the company of the lead insurance investigator and was allegedly abducted and left to die in a forest fire.

There is a great deal of activity around Callister and Blue, and Occam's Razor suggests the simple answer that they are not as detached from the criminal element in Kamloops as they claim.

Now Callister is the centre of another investigation, this time into the murder of one of her classmates. What is she hiding behind sympathy for her past?

Agatha Howard, who is a candidate for mayor in the municipal election, has chosen a colourful person to be her financial officer for the campaign.

Cameron Robinson allegedly asked Callister out on more than one occasion, but his father denies it, saying he had a girlfriend he planned to marry upon graduation.

Mayoral Candidate John Brown has called for Agatha Howard to withdraw from the race, given her and her assistant's disturbing past. Even if they have moved forward, they are not the kind of people Kamloops needs at the helm. He reiterated his call for more law enforcement and security to counter the kind of violence that apparently has followed Callister and Howard.

His daughter, a friend of the murder victim Cameron Robinson, has denied he had any attraction to Callister and certainly was not stalking her.

# Chapter 13
**Friday, October 8**

Blue wanted to kick a chair across the Café. Guests and volunteers stared at him. He cradled his phone to his ear.

"What do you mean the City is cancelling our business license? Didn't they learn anything from the Loop? I haven't received anything in writing, nor an opportunity to appeal."

"Sorry, Blue," Judy said. "I'm just the messenger. I don't want to risk the Loop being caught up again. We've just achieved some kind of balance in the community."

"I'm not closing down. You can fire me to protect the Loop, but too many people depend on the Café to get through the day."

"The fines for operating without a business license can run into the thousands.

"They haven't acted legally to close us down. Until I get something in writing and have a chance to appeal the decision, I am going to continue to do my job."

"Don't make more trouble for yourself."

"Sorry, Judy, I'm not backing down."

He'd barely disconnected the call when Lee phoned.

"The agency is pulling their support. They pay the rent for the Café. Even if you wanted to, there is nothing you can do to keep the place open. If you remain in the building, you will be charged with trespass."

"What does the landlord say? They were all for this."

"They are sympathetic, but they can't afford to defy the City on this."

"I must be able to do something."

"Not unless you can come with another location and a business license. Sorry."

"Shit." Blue hung up and slumped into a chair. "Sorry, folks, the City is shutting us down."

"Can they do that?" Agatha asked.

"No, but they aren't letting that stop them." Blue ground his teeth. "Molly is going to blame herself for this, but it isn't her fault all these rumours have blown up around her.

"We're going to protest this." Agatha slapped the table. "I won't stand silent."

"I can't help. They'll blame the Loop and shut them down too." Blue put his head in his hands. "It's almost enough to drive me to drink again."

"Don't, that goes nowhere good." Agatha walked over and hugged him. "Somehow we will move forward."

"I don't see how." Blue blinked tears from his eyes. "Years of working to make this city a better place count for nothing?"

"It counts for more than you can imagine." Agatha stepped back. "Leave this with me."

***

"I'm resigning." Molly insisted to Agatha, but her voice broke. "I can't drag you down any further." The cold wind blew down the alley chilling her soul.

"I refuse to accept your resignation. That will just let the rumour mongers win." Agatha shook Molly by the shoulders. "Take a break, but I can't do this without you."

"Erica can take over."

"No!" Agatha shouted. "Are you going to admit defeat, admit guilt? That's how they'll read it. We fight back and make more noise than the rumour mongers."

"My past will destroy you."

"If you can't leave your past behind, where does that leave me?" Agatha lowered her head. "I need to fight this, or I'll never be anything more than that crazy homeless lady."

"If you insist, then I'm helping, but I still think I should resign." Molly scrubbed her eyes.

"We'll bypass the rumours and appeal directly to the public." Agatha patted Molly's shoulder. "You'll see.

With Erica's help, they rounded up the regulars at the Café and met in the alley behind the Café.

"We are going to protest at City Hall," Agatha said. "No matter what provocation comes, we will be peaceful."

"We need signs," one said.

"If you want, but nothing inflammatory."

They rescued cardboard from a dumpster and a can of spray paint abandoned by some graffiti artist.

*Innocent until proven guilty.*

*Don't shut us out.*

*Poverty is not a crime.*

Erica posted to her Facebook page and asked people to come join them.

That afternoon, the motley crew headed for City Hall, hardly more than had protested the opening of the Café. They marched with their signs. Some cars honked their horns, but other drivers yelled at them to go home.

"We would if we had one!" Agatha shouted from the steps. "The one safe place we had has been taken from us. Are we going to let them take our other rights away?"

"NO!" the protesters shouted.

"A basic principle of our society is that people are innocent until proven guilty, yet we are treated as guilty just because we are poor, because we are homeless. We are still citizens of this country no matter how the City may treat us."

A security guard came out of City Hall waving his arms.

"You can't be here."

"You are denying our legal right to protest?" Agatha pointed to where a tv station van parked and cameras were aimed at them. "We aren't blocking access to the City Hall, and it is public property."

"If you won't leave, we'll call the police."

"Do that." Agatha crossed her arms. "Let them come and arrest us."

The protest gathered more people as supporters of the Loop and the Café heard the news.

The following day, counter-protesters also gathered and shouted that criminals shouldn't be allowed on the streets.

"Who are the criminals?" Agatha responded. "We haven't been convicted in any court but public opinion. You are the ones trying to deny us our basic rights."

The police showed up and formed a line between the two protests and kept an uneasy peace.

***

Behind the reporter, the two groups marched and tried to shout each other down.

"An election in Kamloops, BC has spilled out onto the streets as protesters march on City Hall. It is the third day of protest and counter-protest. Rumours have flown about the pasts of one candidate and her financial officer, but nothing has been substantiated.

"Agatha Howard is claiming they have been found guilty without any trial or appeal. A well-used drop-in shelter provided something to do throughout the day for many homeless in downtown Kamloops. A similar program on the North Shore generated backlash from the businesses in the neighbourhood, but a compromise was reached which kept the Loop open and offering a wide range of services from food to medical care, including a safe injection site.

"The Lived Experience Community, who runs the Loop is advocating for safe supply in response to the ongoing opioid crisis which has caused more deaths than the pandemic in the province.

"John Brown, another candidate for mayor, insists that agencies like the Loop and the Café coddle people who might otherwise turn their lives around."

The reporter waited for his camera person to signal he was off the air. "Let's get inside where it's warm.

***

Agatha met the leaders of the protest in the alley behind the Café on the morning of the fourth day. The wind was cold, but they were used to the cold.

"We have to keep going until the City breaks down. They can't ignore us forever. The eyes of the world are on us."

She looked around at the small crowd. Some were shining with excitement, but others, like Molly, looked drained by the experience.

Molly hugged herself. "The protests have spilled over to the Loop. I have a bad feeling about all this. It isn't going to end well."

"The cameras are rolling. No one is going to do anything with the nation watching." Agatha told her. "This could be the day they break. It will be okay."

A group of people with black balaclavas and sunglasses approached from one end of the alley.

When Agatha turned to look, another group was walking toward them from the other end. She looked for an escape, but as if on a signal, the groups charged. Her people fought to defend themselves against those wielding baseball bats and crowbars.

Molly took a position in front of Agatha, determined to protect her. Some of the homeless protesters broke free and fled to the street at the end of the alley, but that left the rest outnumbered by the attackers. Two of them converged on Molly. She sidestepped a bat and moved in close and threw the person against the wall of the one-time Café. The attacker with the crowbar circled looking for an opportunity.

Another black-masked crowbar wielder jumped at Molly from behind. Agatha threw herself forward and pushed Molly out of the way. Blinding pain struck Agatha's head, then shoulder. She fell to the pavement. The last thing she saw was two people charging Molly.

***

Molly dodged another attack, then caught the next person's sleeve and tossed them hard on the pavement. A bat hit her ribs, and she screamed with the pain and backed against the wall. Sirens wailed, approaching quickly.

"Bug out!" One of the people in black shouted. The crowd dispersed, leaving moaning protesters on the pavement. Molly spotted Agatha lying face down with blood pouring from her head.

"No!" She staggered over and tried to decide what to do. A crease ran down the side of Agatha's head, and Molly didn't want to make things worse.

A police car pulled into the alley and two cops got out, hands on their holsters.

"Call an ambulance!" Molly screamed as her ribs flared in complaint, but she didn't care. One of the officers spoke into her radio. More sirens approached.

Sergeant Ferguson climbed out of one of the newly arrived cars. "Just can't stay out of trouble can you, Callister."

"You're blaming me for this?" Molly tried to shout, but it came out as a harsh whisper. She coughed and spat blood, hitting Ferguson's shoes.

"Spitting on a police officer is assault."

"If she's coughing blood, she needs an ambulance." Hassim put a hand on Ferguson's arm. "You can charge her later if she survives."

The ambulance arrived and the paramedics crowded around Agatha. They put a collar on her and carefully lifted her onto a stretcher.

Molly was going to demand to ride with Agatha but couldn't get air to speak. A paramedic shouted, and she was lifted onto a stretcher and an oxygen mask fitted over her face.

***

Ferguson rounded on Hassim. "Don't you ever get in my way."

"You can arrest her later," Hassim replied, "but the news cameras are rolling, and unless you want to be on tonight's news for her dying in your custody, you'll shut up."

Ferguson wanted to say a lot more, but reporters had followed the sirens and were filming from outside the line of cars. He could imagine what the reports would say. He swore and walked over to the nearest reporter.

"Did you get any footage of the fight?"

"No, we got here after the action was over. Who was in the ambulance?"

"I can't comment on that now."

"What happened here?" The mic was pointed at him, so Ferguson didn't say what he wanted to.

"We don't know yet. We have to interview the witnesses. You will know when we have something to report." His car was blocked in, so he grabbed one of the officers on the outside of the scrum and got her to drive him to the RIH.

"What a fricking mess."

# Chapter 14

Ferg— Sergeant Ferguson came up to the hospital and talked to her, seeming almost sympathetic, though anger radiated off him.

"They were wearing balaclavas or masks and sunglasses. I couldn't give you much of a description. One or two of them will be aching as our people got a few blows in before they broke."

"Did you get any shots in?"

"I'm in judo. I don't do punches and kicks much, but I threw a couple, one into a wall and the other on the ground. I didn't see how they landed as one of them got me with a baseball bat."

"Were they targeting Agatha Howard?"

"She pushed me out of the way of a crowbar, I'm not sure they meant to cause such a serious injury."

"Maybe they were targeting you?"

"I don't think so. It felt like a big mob, but I don't know if there were more than eight or ten of them."

"Is this shit storm connected to Cameron Robinson?" He leaned forward as he asked.

"I wouldn't know; none of them said anything. My guess is they wanted us to give up the protest."

"Makes sense." Sergeant Ferguson stood up. "Thanks for talking to me."

Soon after that, she'd been sent home.

Molly moved around the apartment gingerly. Her cracked ribs made breathing painful, but even so, she was more worried about Agatha who was still unconscious after surgery to relieve pressure on her brain.

Molly turned on the news as a distraction from her pain.

The mayoral candidates all decried the violence, but John Brown couldn't resist blaming the victims for creating the situation. Molly expected that. What made her angry was that all of them wrote off Agatha as a candidate. They'd never taken her seriously. Other protests continued with spokespeople talking about Agatha as a martyr.

"She's not dead, and she wouldn't quit." Molly snarled at the TV.

"What can you do about it?" Blue sighed. "She's in a coma in the hospital. She shook up the election and made it the most interesting one in decades."

"I'm going to do what she planned. Get out in the streets and talk to people."

"Are you sure that's wise? You aren't exactly a hundred percent."

"The doctor said it was important to move around and breathe normally. Talking with people will help both."

"Okay, but I'm coming with you." Blue insisted. "We still don't know the purpose of the attack."

*** 

Molly bundled up the next day and headed to Victoria Street. with Blue. Her ribs still hurt, but the pain was manageable. She forced herself to take deep breaths though each one twinged uncomfortably.

She wore her 'Agatha for Mayor' button.

"What are your concerns for the municipal election?" Molly asked everyone who slowed down to offer sympathy for Agatha's injury. Blue lurked in the background

"Crime and violence are getting worse."

"It is," Molly said, "but why do you think so?"

"Look at the fight between the protesters. That wouldn't have happened if she hadn't made such a fuss about that place closing."

Again and again, no matter how sympathetic the person started, most ended up blaming Agatha and the protest for the violence.

"How so?" Molly started asking. Answers ranged from because those people should know their place to a deer in the headlights look. In the middle were a variety of suggestions that since the counter-protest was anti-crime, Agatha's protest was somehow pro-crime

"All they wanted was a warm place to have a cup of coffee and some socializing" became her next line. "Can you blame them?" Molly didn't have to fake the shiver from the cold.

"Can't they go to a coffee shop like the rest of us?"

"They wish they could, but even if someone like you gave them the money for a coffee, would they be welcome to sit through the day talking with friends?

"They should keep cleaner and look more presentable," was one rebuff.

"How? There aren't enough washrooms and showers available for them to stay clean, and new clothes are expensive. I've been there."

"But you don't look homeless."

"I was lucky and got free instead of dying, but it was a close thing. Besides, it isn't just the homeless who used the Café, but seniors on a tight budget or who are just lonely."

It was exhausting and frustrating. Too many people who had never experienced homelessness of any kind couldn't get their minds around the idea that most of those on the street didn't choose to live rough and weren't lazy.

When she couldn't take the pain and cold anymore, Molly retreated to a coffee shop and held different conversations.

At the end of the day, she'd heard a bewildering number of things people were worried about beyond crime and violence. There was the ever-increasing lack of affordable housing, the forest fires and floods which were becoming more common. When asked for solutions responses ranged from 'that's your job' to versions of 'what we are already doing, but make it work.'

Molly finally returned home and flopped on the couch, squealing at the pain in her ribs.

"I don't know what to do next."

"What did Agatha do?"

"She somehow organized it into something she could create policy around."

"You don't need to start from scratch, Agatha had some pretty solid suggestions."

Molly dragged herself up, fetched her bag with Agatha's notes and buried herself in them. She was missing classes at university but couldn't face sitting still for hours with her ribs throbbing.

***

**Sunday, October 10**

Molly bundled up and went out on the street again to where Erica was keeping the protest going. Erica had a black eye and felt guilty for not protecting Agatha.

"I couldn't either," Molly said. "Now we have to carry on. The hospital said her vital signs are good, and they don't think she'll have much damage from the injury.

John Brown came over.

"I'm so sorry to hear about Agatha, but you aren't doing her any favours."

"I'm going to keep working on the campaign until she tells me to stop."

"What if she doesn't wake up?"

"I'm going to continue to work," Molly said. "Excuse me." She talked to each person protesting on behalf of the Café.

"The people on that side aren't the enemy; they're just people trying to figure out life. They're scared, but it is more comfortable to be angry."

Molly wandered over to the other protest.

"What are you doing here?" A man got in her face.

"Just here to talk." Molly squashed her anger. "I want to hear all sides of the issue. Marching around shouting at each other isn't working."

"Get out of here or I'll put you in the bed next to that nutcase."

"Don't be rude," said a grey-haired woman who reminded her of the Pointy Shoes ladies. "The girl is willing to listen."

"Look, you…"

"Unless you plan to threaten me too, young man, be quiet." The woman didn't back down, though he was bigger and much taller. "We need more young people like her."

"You mean hookers and killers?" The man sneered.

"People who have worked hard to improve themselves. It doesn't matter where they come from." She turned to Molly. "You didn't kill that poor boy, did you?"

"No."

"What else is she going to say?" The man shouted.

"Do be quiet; I'm trying to have a conversation here." She led Molly to the side where it was less frenetic. Another woman and a man followed her. The big man disappeared.

"We need to do something about crime and violence." The man put his hands behind his back.

"We do indeed," Molly replied and smiled at the man's shock. "None of the people over there want crime and violence. They've probably lived through a lot more of it than you have. They've been beaten, robbed, and pushed out of anywhere that felt safe. All they want is a warm place where they don't have to worry about things."

"Don't we all?" the man said. "I've worked hard for what I have. Why should they just get life handed to them? I'm not against helping the poor, but we can't baby them. I'm here because I believe they should be responsible for their own lives."

Molly pointed at the different sides. "It's like children yelling 'is not' 'is too' until they forget what the argument is about."

"So what would you suggest?" the other woman asked.

"How about we fight crime, not people."

"What do you mean by that?" The grey-haired woman tilted her head.

"Poverty is a root cause of crime. Desperate, hungry people will act out in ways our society doesn't accept. If they weren't poor, if they had a warm home and food to eat, they wouldn't look much different than you."

"Them?" The man looked offended.

"Yes." Molly went to cross her arms and decided against it. "We are all working for the same thing, a just society where people can be safe and happy."

"Like that will ever happen." The man crossed his arms and frowned. "There are too many lazy people in the world."

"Aren't we all a bit lazy?" Molly gave up and hugged her ribs. "Wouldn't we all like life to be easier?"

"Are you okay?" The other woman asked.

"My ribs were broken with a baseball bat." Molly winced as if talking about it made the pain worse. "In the same attack that put my boss, my friend in the hospital."

"You're the one who was on the radio." The man poised as if to run.

"That's me, Molly Callister, scars and all."

"Oh dear, that's terrible." The grey-haired woman reached out to hug her, then pulled back. "I heard the interview. Such a hard life for someone so young."

"I'm not that unusual." Molly shrugged and winced again. "There are more people out there like me than I care to think."

"But surely you had to work hard to break free," the man said.

"I had the luck to have my hard work pay off. Many girls work as hard and still end up dead in back alleys. That's why places like the Café and the Loop are so important: they increase the chances of recovery."

"I see." The man turned and walked back to the counter-protest, but he didn't start chanting slogans again.

John Brown stalked over to Molly.

"What do you think you are doing?"

"My job, Mr. Brown."

"It isn't your job."

"It is everyone's job."

"You're a reprobate. People like you can't change. You shouldn't be here with decent people. You probably killed that poor young man." He was shouting now.

Molly turned and walked away.

"I haven't finished talking to you." John Brown yelled.

She lifted a finger to him, then grinned. The man sputtered behind her, but she melted into the crowd of protesters without looking back.

***

## Monday, October 11

Blue stared at Judy in her office at the Loop.

"They want us to reopen?"

"In a limited capacity, but yes." Judy rubbed her forehead. "I finally came to an agreement with the City brass. I think they want all the noise to go away."

"I will get right on it."

"Part of the deal is the protest stops. They're finding it hard to work with the ruckus outside."

"I'll swing by and let Erica know."

"And they want Molly to stop her campaigning."

"That's beyond my control." Blue stood up. "I should get to the protest, make more ruckus until they come to their senses."

"That's pretty much what I thought you'd say." Judy sighed. "I will let them know that if they back off Molly, I won't go to the press about them interfering with her charter rights. Go get the Café up and running. The weather isn't getting any warmer."

# Chapter 15

Molly sat in a corner of the Café reading the notes from Agatha and warming up for another walk on Victoria. Erica and her crew scrubbed the Café while Blue checked the inventory in the kitchen. They were low on everything since he'd given all the food away when the place was closed.

Word on the street had gotten out that they were opening again. Anyone who showed up at the door was put to work, whether it was cleaning or making PB&J sandwiches. The Café echoed with conversation and laughter.

Blue hadn't made any official announcement, hoping to avoid backlash. Without the protest at City Hall, the anti-crime people had declared themselves victorious and retreated to warm homes, bars, and restaurants.

The door opened and Lee slipped in.

"Looking good." She accepted a cup of coffee and sat with Molly out of the way of the workers. "Turns out the funders weren't happy with the idea of the Café being arbitrarily closed. There was some pressure on the agency and the City to rectify the situation. Apparently, someone sent a complaint to the feds that the City was playing politics with the government's money."

"Can't say that I'm surprised, what with demonstrations popping up all over the place demanding better treatment of the homeless." Molly looked up from her work. "I'm hoping the violence trying to shut down the pro-Café protest had something to do with it too."

"Most of the national news sources played it down as a group of overly enthusiastic anti-crime people. Ironic given that they protested crime by committing one."

"Probably saw themselves as heroes protecting the city." Molly sighed and rubbed her side. "When you equate homelessness with criminal, it is easy to justify a bit of intimidation 'for the greater good.' I had better get back onto the street before I freeze up completely." She didn't feel like carrying the heavy bag with her and asked Erica to put it in Blue's office.

Outside the wind was chilly and blowing along Victoria. Molly headed for City Hall. It was a good place to talk to people coming out of the building."

"It isn't so much a matter of whether there should be a place like the Café, but where it should be." A woman in a long puffy coat said. "There is always an effect on neighbouring businesses. We learned that on Tranquille. I'm on the Business Improvement Association."

"Have you quantified the effects, or it is self-reported through complaints?"

"We haven't done a study on the numbers, but the incidences of theft and vandalism did increase on Tranquille when the Loop began operation."

"What about after they closed?" Molly asked, wishing for a puffy coat of her own.

"I have no idea."

"Thanks for your time." Molly caught sight of a man in a black mask and dark glasses, and her heart banged until he wandered away. She walked east along Victoria in the opposite direction of the black mask

People weren't as willing to stop in the chill wind, but a few talked with her while waiting for traffic lights. Most weren't interested in the election. In fact, a few hadn't known of it until Molly mentioned it. She dropped into the Smorgasbord as much to warm up as to talk to the few people drinking coffee. On the way back, someone bumped into her, spilling her take-out coffee all over her jacket.

Cursing, she headed for the bus exchange on Landsdowne. She kept glimpsing men in black masks but put it down to a reaction to the attack. No one would bother her on the street. She climbed onto the number two bus and only then realized that she'd left her notes and keys in her bag at the Café, not to mention her wallet with her bus pass. Apologizing to the driver, she got back off and headed for the Café.

She saw more people with the black masks and wondered when they got so popular. Maybe someone had a sale on the black ones. Molly was able to calm her nerves until she saw one with dark glasses who pushed away from the wall and walked toward her. She ducked through the crowd and across the street, prompting a driver to honk their horn at her. When she glanced back, the man waved at her.

Surely it was her imagination, but was he leering at her? Molly arrived at the Café out of breath and shivering. Lee had left, so she picked up her bag and was started to leave but decided at the last minute to work until the Café closed and Blue could go home with her.

***

"Agatha Howard is awake," Hassim informed Ferguson. "I'm going to go up and see if she is up to talking a bit.

"I doubt she'll be able to add much to the picture." Ferguson didn't look up from his paperwork. "But we need to be thorough."

Hassim drove up to the RIH and headed to the ward where, according to the latest information she'd got from the hospital, Agatha Howard was resting quietly. Masked people walked past, even more nameless and detached than before the pandemic.

Up in the ICU, Hassim got the okay to talk to Howard for a few minutes.

"She's still groggy from the painkillers." The nurse escorted him to her bedside.

"Agatha, someone here to see you."

Agatha's eyes opened and took a moment to focus on Hassim.

"Ms. Howard, I'm Sergeant Hassim. I'd like to ask you a few questions about the attack on you and the others in the alley."

"Molly, she all right?"

"Yes, she got away with just cracked ribs."

"I thought they were going to kill…" Agatha trailed off as her eyes closed.

"Thank you." Hasim left her card on the table beside the bed.

"Well?" the nurse asked.

"Fell asleep in the middle of her second sentence."

"Asking about Molly?"

"Yes, is she having memory issues?"

"Could be a result of the meds." The nurse shook her head.

"Thanks, I left a card in case she wanted to talk to me more."

"All right, I'll let the duty nurse know.

Hassim headed back to the station and found Ferguson looking at old cases from Vancouver.

"First thing the woman says is 'Molly, she all right?'"

Ferguson grunted.

"What if Callister isn't the perp but the target?"

"Vancouver PD contacted us. They have a couple of cases similar enough to ours to raise a flag."

"What?"

"Nine years back a presumed john found with pants around his ankles, stab wound to the heart. No hesitation, shirt over his face."

"That would make Callister about fifteen."

"And still in school, sometimes at least."

"You said a couple."

"The other two years later." Ferguson tapped the screen. "Ruled self-defence, the killer was under-age. Victim a known pimp, and a nasty one too. Records sealed blah, blah, blah."

"What do a john, a pimp, and a clean-cut student have in common?"

"Maybe they were trying to stick their thing where it didn't belong." Ferguson swivelled to look at Hassim "Checked on the kid's girlfriend. According to the parents, very nice but a bit jealous."

"Maybe worth a chat."

"Handle with kid gloves. There's politics around this one. Inspector says to stay clear unless the evidence mounts. Not likely to be the killer. She is twenty-three, making her fourteen when the first murder happened."

"Right," Hassim shrugged, "if there even is a connection. A single stab wound and pants around the knees is stretching it a bit."

"Callister said Robinson was harassing her for a date. Maybe she was telling the truth. Reputations always get a polish after death."

"Howard thought someone was going to kill Callister."

"None of the other witnesses said anything, not even Callister." Ferguson frowned. "I'm not giving her a pass yet. There's still her jacket and the text she claimed she got, that Blue denied."

"Maybe we should get a warrant and check her phone. Should have done that right off," she muttered.

"We would have had to show cause, and she was just a material witness then."

"You could have charged her. We've arrested people on less."

"Maybe after we found the jacket, but she tied us in knots in that interview." Ferguson's frown deepened

"Did you get the lab to check the shirt against the jacket?"

"Undetermined. The shirt was bloody enough it might have stains from under the jacket."

"Where are we with the case then?" Hassim raised an eyebrow.

"Damned if I know."

"How about if I ask pretty please if we can look at the phone to confirm her story?" Hassim made puppy eyes at Ferguson.

"Go ahead if you want. If she's smart, she'll tell you where to go."

"Worth a try then." Hassim got up. "That Café will still be open. I can catch Blue before it closes and get a message to her."

Rain speckled the windshield as Hassim drove to the Café and parked out front. She'd walked in before considering what kind of welcome she'd get.

"What do you want?" A tough-looking woman got in Hassim's way. She was one of the ones injured in the brawl in the alley.

"Just a friendly message for Molly." Hassim smiled and tried to look unthreatening. Difficult with thirty pounds of equipment hanging off her.

"Might as well let her in, Erica," Molly called from a corner.

Erica stepped aside and went back to work.

154

"Hello, Molly." Hassim settled herself across from the girl. Paper covered the table.

"I'd offer you coffee, but I don't want to mess up my work."

"School work?"

"Election." Molly rolled her eyes. "School is a walk in the park compared to this. But you didn't come here to talk policy."

"In your statement, you said you received a text from Blue asking you to meet him."

"I did."

"We'd like to check your phone to confirm that." Hassim half hoped Callister would pull the phone out right away, even to show her the text on the screen.

"Didn't you get the complaint I filed?" Molly frowned. "My phone bricked while it was in your custody. I know it was working because I had to power It down before they'd store it."

"It isn't working?"

"I sent it to Conrad to have it checked out. I've been without a phone all week." Molly stood. "Wait here." She went into the back, then came out. "I've left a message with him to call me."

"You said you filled out a complaint form?"

"Yeah, when I was picking up my stuff."

"Any other issues with your belongings?

"No. I'll call you when I hear from Conrad." Molly leaned forward. "Any word on the SOB's who hurt Agatha?"

"Nothing solid." Hassim sighed and took a flyer. "You ever live in Vancouver?"

"Fuck no." Molly sat back and pushed her chair away from the table. "Haven't you done your homework? The gang I escaped tried to sell me down to Vancouver. That was a death sentence. Shit, even the media got that piece right."

"I look forward to your call." Hassim made her escape. Callister couldn't have reacted more strongly if she'd pulled her gun on the girl. She drove back to the station and pulled up Molly Callister as the victim of a crime, a different database from criminal records. Reading it made her skin crawl.

She called Ferguson. "Look up Molly Callister as the victim of crime in the past four years. It explains a few things." Then she went to processing and looked for the complaint form. As she'd expected it was buried in the in-basket. Since Callister mentioned the media, Hassim did a search for news. It was informative reading.

***

Molly was watching the news when Blue came in and handed her his phone.

"Ciara."

She nodded at him and took the phone.

"Hi."

"I've been messaging you forever," Ciara said.

"Sorry," Molly went to her computer and booted it up. Notifications scrolled down the screen. "I got busy with the campaign, then my phone died."

"You didn't even check your computer?"

"Never thought of it. I haven't been at school lately."

"You told me not to skip classes."

"I did, but I got hurt and couldn't sit in class."

"You still have to do the work." Ciara sounded like her grandmother.

"You're right. I'll have a lot of catching up to do."

"You should have called and said you were hurt."

"Yup." Molly sighed. "I'm sorry."

"I saw some news." Ciara stopped and Molly pictured the young girl on the edge of tears.

"There has been some rough stuff going on. It's part of the election."

"They said you maybe killed someone. I got in a fight at school over that. I said you'd never." Ciara sounded determined.

"Fighting isn't good."

"I had to. I won't let anyone dis you."

"How many days' suspension?"

"Grandma told me I had to work as hard as I would at school. The house has never been so clean." Ciara said.

"Thanks for the support, Ciara." Molly wiped an eye. "I know how you feel about housework. I didn't kill anyone, but I did find the body of one of my classmates, and he had been murdered. The police had a lot of questions."

"That sounds tough."

"You know it. I spent a day in the cells. Let me tell you, that's worse than detention. Almost as bad as housework."

"Are you going to come over and visit?"

"When the election is done, another five days. Maybe your grandma will let you help at the debate on Friday."

"I'll ask her. Check your messages though."

"I will."

## John Brown for Mayor Group

JB [can you believe they opened that place again?]

DH [maybe we should shut them down ourselves.]

JB [as much as I'd like to, illegal actions won't help us.]

158

DH [give it time and there will be something. You'll see.]

***

The latest polls put Agatha Howard in third place... Though she is presently in hospital recovering from a brawl behind the Café, her financial officer has maintained and even expanded the campaign... John Brown has slipped from fourth to last place...

In other news, the City, in a surprise move, announced the reopening of the Café on Victoria Street. They state that provisions have been put in place including increased staffing, and the outreach will encourage people to meet there instead of on the street or in back alleys. Though the Loop on Tranquille had some difficult times with optics and gathering outside the building, lessons learned have been applied to the Café.

# Chapter 16
**Tuesday, October 12**

The kitchen at the Café had finally met inspection so they could cook hot meals. Tad from the Loop was coming over to start as chef. Blue liked the young man; he worked hard and kept the kitchen immaculately clean. Blue suspected he had a bit of a crush on Molly. That was fine as long as it didn't get in the way of the Café's work.

Today's meal was simple mac and cheese. Or it would have been simple if it wasn't Tad doing the cooking. He managed to create meals worthy of a fine restaurant from whatever donations came in.

Blue got off the bus and headed to the Café to open up. The front was covered with red paint.

'Fucking murderers' streaked like blood down the front window. Blue called Erica.

"We'll need your crew as soon as possible. Someone's decorated our front window. I'm going to check the back. Assume they've tagged the bricks as well." He hoped she picked up the message soon. As he expected, the back of the building was covered with more graffiti with outlines of bodies on the pavement of the back alley.

Someone had been kicking on the back door. Before the Café had opened, Blue had swapped the normal screws out for four-inch deck screws. They would have had to break the wall, not just the door frame.

He unlocked the door and walked into the back of the Café, half expecting chaos and disaster, but the inside was in good shape except for cracks in the drywall around the door.

The wood replacing the glass of the broken window had taken a beating as well, but again the long screws had held up. He was surprised they hadn't broken the big front window.

Erica showed up a few minutes later steaming mad, hauling cleaning supplies in a grocery cart.

"I've made a few calls. I'll be out front." She grabbed some rags and a brush along with paint cleaner. She and some others spent time erasing the more offensive graffiti around Kamloops. Blue doubted that anyone noticed.

"Blue, the news people are out front."

Blue sighed and walked through the Café to join Erica at the front. A small crowd had gathered along with the news van.

"Don't let them interfere with your work. I'll take care of the talking." Erica nodded and set to removing the paint from the window and the frames.

"As you can see, you've caught us in the midst of cleaning up." Blue smiled at the reporter. "If you're going to do a report, kindly show Erica cleaning up the mess."

"Aren't you angry about this?" The reporter held her mic out.

"Sure, but angry doesn't deal with the situation." Blue shrugged. "It isn't the first time our building has been hit with graffiti. We have a procedure for dealing with the mess. The landlord shouldn't have to the be ones bearing the cost of cleanup."

"Who do you think did this?" The reporter pushed the mic closer to him.

"I don't want to speculate, but obviously the message is counter to what we stand for. The Café is a warm place for anyone to drop in for a coffee and conversation."

"There has been a lot of controversy surrounding the opening of the Café."

"Of course." Blue smiled. "There are those who see a homeless person and immediately assume they are an addict and petty criminal, so the idea of people without homes or precarious housing situations gathering in one place is scary. The truth is the percentage of criminals among the homeless is not much more than in the general population. Most of the effort goes to surviving from day to day."

"So you're saying no criminals are using your Café?"

Blue laughed. "Can you say there are no criminals eating in your high-end restaurants? Criminals don't look any different than you or I."

More of Erica's crew had arrived, and the paint was vanishing faster than Blue had expected.

"Feel free to stop by later in the day and check out the end result of the cleanup."

The news crew packed up, and the crowd dispersed. Blue went back inside. The Café was already smelling good, and his stomach growled. He checked in the kitchen.

"Saw the mess on the way in," Tad said. "Figured you'd have it handled, and I needed to get onto food. Coffee is brewed."

"Good work, Tad."

***

Molly finished walking Harley and put her in the apartment. She double-checked the door to be sure it caught properly. It had been acting up in the colder weather. Harley wouldn't leave the place, but it disconcerted people to walk by and see the big black dog guarding the door.

She ran down the stairs and reached the bus stop just in time to catch her ride. She would have pulled out her phone, but she still hadn't replaced it. Maybe Conrad would have news for her soon.

The bus dropped her on Seymour, and she walked to the Café.

After the events of the last weeks, she went the long way around to the front and said hello to Erica on the way in. She went to the corner table she'd claimed as an office.

"Trouble last night?" She said as someone put coffee on the table beside her.

"Blue found a ton of graffiti this morning." Tad's voice startled her.

"Sorry, I thought you were Blue."

Tad blushed and escaped back to the kitchen.

Molly shook her head and went to work. She sipped at the coffee. When had Tad learned how she drank her coffee? The work pulled her in, and she put it out of her mind. The next and final debate was on the fourteenth, only two days away. Agatha was conscious, sort of, but wouldn't be in shape to speak at the debate. Molly was going to take her place. That meant more preparation than she had done yet for any essay or class. Agatha was depending on her.

She wished she had heard Agatha's entire speech at the earlier debate. Blue had talked to her about it, so she was confident she wouldn't contradict anything her boss said.

"You have a moment?" Naomi stood across the table. "I'd like to do a blog post about this place. I'm interviewing people who hang out here."

Molly looked up and waved to the empty chair. "Sure, have a seat. You want a coffee?"

"Thanks, but no. I've had plenty already." Naomi pulled out a notepad. "Now, what is all the work you have here?"

"The mayoral debate is in two days. I need to be ready." Molly waved a hand at the paper-covered table.

"But with Agatha in the hospital…"

"I don't intend to leave her work hanging in the wind." Molly set her chin stubbornly.

"Does City Hall know you are planning to be there?"

"They should - I've been campaigning hard enough - but I've left messages for the organizers saying that Agatha will be represented. From what I've heard, two of the candidates are against me taking her place."

"Let me guess, one of them is John Brown."

"Probably." Molly sipped at her coffee. "They didn't say. It is up to the sitting mayor to break the tie. My source is thinking he will err on the side of inclusivity."

"Your source?" Naomi raised an eyebrow. "Now you're sounding like a journalist."

Molly laughed.

"Why do your work here? Wouldn't it be quieter at home?"

"I feel safe here." Molly looked around. "Everyone is here for warmth and company. It isn't that there aren't any arguments or problems here, but that's part of the package. Kamloops could do worse than imitate the atmosphere here."

"Don't know how many votes you'd get for that." Naomi looked around the room.

"I'm tempted to put it in my speech, just to see their faces."

"I'll be there," Naomi leaned forward, "cheering you on. Now, back to the Café. I don't want to question your word, but I know Blue is here most of the time and I'd imagine that is very comforting."

"It is, but I think it would be the same if he was at a meeting. Blue coordinates the Café, but it is a team of people who do the work of welcoming and keeping the peace." Molly sighed and shook her head. "I saw some of that in the news report from this morning. It was like Blue was articulating what Erica and the others live through at the Café and, honestly, outside in the city as well."

"You feel safe here, but you still walk Victoria Street."

"That is where the people are. The pulse of Kamloops; I need to listen to that. The risk is less than I feel. It is easy for me to think myself into fear." Molly ignored her speeding heartbeat.

"Just be careful you don't ignore a real threat."

"It's hard. I found Cameron, then the attack that put Agatha in the hospital, but I can't believe that's the norm, or I'd never leave my apartment." Molly fought back the shudder that tried to run down her spine.

"Thanks for the talk. Is there anything you don't want me to quote?" Naomi put her pad away.

"Don't say anything about Kamloops needing to be like the Café."

"Gotcha." Naomi got up and went over to another table where three older men were playing cards.

"You need more coffee?" Tad stood with a cup in his hand.

"Thanks." Molly accepted the cup.

"Molly." Tad cleared his throat. "Do you like movies?"

"Most of the time," Molly said.

"There is a good show at the Paramount." He blushed and Molly thought he would bolt for the kitchen, but he took a breath. "Would you like to go with me?"

"I'm sort of tied up this week." Tad's face fell. "But next week I would be delighted."

He brightened. "I'm not sure what's on next week, but the movie's at seven, so I can pick you up at 6:30?"

"How about Tuesday's show?"

"Sure." He almost skipped back to the kitchen.

Molly grinned. She was glad he'd built up the courage to ask. With school and Covid, she hadn't had much of a social life in the past couple years.

***

Molly hunched against the cold and damp. Few people were on the street, but she talked to Nan, a woman who had a tiny apartment but was more comfortable on the street.

"Fall weather." Nan made a face. "Hate it."

"Should stop in at the Café and warm up."

"Might do." Nan shrugged. "How's your mayor lady?"

"Doing better, talked to her last night on the phone. She's a tough one."

"Sure is, you think mayoring is easier than running a thrift shop?"

"Don't know, but running for mayor is harder than school."

Nan laughed and the echoes lightened the chill for a moment.

"Listen, lass, the street's in an ugly mood. It don't like blood being shed. You be careful. Keep your guardian spirit close."

"Guardian spirit?"

"Don't know, just what comes to me." Nan hugged Molly. "Just be safe. The street don't wanna lose you."

"Thanks, Nan."

The woman walked away down the street, and Molly shivered. Nan was always a little spooky, but something about the nearly deserted street made it feel colder.

She ducked into a coffee shop and hugged herself. Her ribs ached.

"You're that Agatha's girl." The only man in the shop glared at her. "Some people don't know when to stay down."

"None of that here." The girl behind the counter glowered at the man. "Everyone is welcome here, unless they cause trouble."

"You gonna stop me, girlie? The man got up and loomed over the counter.

"Do you have any hobbies aside from threatening girls?" Molly asked and readied herself to intervene.

"Why should I listen to some chickie with blood on her hands?"

"If you're so sure I'm a stone-cold killer, do you really want to get me angry?" Molly didn't have to fake the ice in her voice. She almost wanted him to attack her so she could take him down.

"You think you're tough with that judo shit. It ain't gonna help when the hammer falls."

"We'll see. Were you swinging a bat or a crowbar, mister?"

"Wouldn't you like to know?" He leered at her and crowded Molly. She put a table between them.

"Everything all right, Molly?" Tad walked in the door.

"Just peachy, Tad." She hadn't noticed just how tall and solid he was.

"Stay out of it, kid." The man turned to snarl at Tad.

"Like hell." Tad moved to stand between Molly and the man, who clenched his fists tighter.

Flashing lights interrupted them before they came to blows, and Constable Post came in the door, hand on his holster.

"Good afternoon, Constable Post," Molly said. "Good to see you again."

"How's things?" The officer swept the room with his gaze.

"Tense." Molly deliberately relaxed and stepped back to lean against the counter. "This gentleman was just telling me how he enjoyed hitting people with a baseball bat. Compensating, I guess."

The man surged toward Molly. Tad and Constable Post both put out their hands to stop him. He took a swing at Tad who caught the man's fist and held it.

"I don't like violence," Tad stared into the man's eyes, "but I'll make an exception for you."

"I could tear you to pieces and not break a sweat." He yanked his hand from Tad's grip, and his elbow hit Constable Post in the face.

The big officer caught the man's arm and twisted. Before the guy could resist, he was cuffed.

"Uttering threats, assaulting a police officer, disturbing the peace, and Sergeant Ferguson will want to have a word with you about that bat."

"Fuck you, I'm not saying a thing."

"We'll see." Constable Post took the man's arm. "You are under arrest" He gave the man his rights. "You going to be all right, Molly?"

"Tad's here; I'll be fine."

Tad straightened and the back of his neck reddened.

"You, miss?" Constable Post asked the girl behind the counter.

"My boss is on the way. I'm good." She didn't look happy.

The officer nodded and dragged the man out the door.

"Smart thinking to call the police while he was distracted."

The girl behind the counter started shaking.

"Come and sit down before you fall over." Molly went behind the counter and led the girl out to one of the tables.

"But…"

"We'll stay until your boss gets here."

They didn't have to wait long. She thanked Molly and Tad, then sat with the girl.

"There are supposed to be two people on at all times." The boss frowned.

"Shani called in sick at the last minute. It wasn't busy…"

Another officer arrived to take statements taking care to talk to each out of earshot of the others. When they were done Molly led Tad out the door.

"Thanks, how did you know I needed help?"

"Nan told me."

"I'll have to give her an extra hug next time I see her."

As they walked back to the Café, Tad took her hand.

172

"You're shaking."

"Reaction." Molly squeezed his hand. "I'll be fine, now."

***

Sergeant Ferguson leaned against the wall in the interview room.

"I heard you're a tough guy, Hank."

"You have nothing to hold me."

"So you say." Ferguson opened the file in his hand. "It's not the first time you've been here, is it? I see you've graduated to assaulting a police officer."

"He shoulda know better than to stand behind me."

"We're picking up a few of your buddies. Let them know you spilled the beans on that shindig that put Ms. Howard in hospital. Makes you an accessory to attempted murder." Ferguson flipped through the file.

"Should have stayed out of the way."

"Really? So you *were* aiming for Ms. Callister." Ferguson tapped the file against his leg. "Aggravated assault with intent. Conspiracy too, since you planned the attack. Can't hardly claim you just stumbled into a brawl when you're carrying weapons."

"I was talking about the coffee shop. She had to butt in and throw her weight around."

"But you recognized her."

"So what?"

"Means you've seen her before." Ferguson paced the room. "Knew about her judo, too."

"You can't prove I was there."

"Not yet. When your friends get here it will be a race to see who makes the deal first." Ferguson headed for the door, then spun and came back. "Look, I understand you didn't mean for it to go that far. You were supposed to just shake 'em up, but it got out of hand."

"That's for damned sure." Hank slumped. "I didn't plan it."

Ferguson paused. "Really?"

"Some chick put us up to it."

"You got a name?"

"Nah, she was masked and all."

"Not good enough." Ferguson shrugged. "Might as well send you down for it. Who swung the crowbar?"

"Sure as hell wasn't me." Hank leaned back. "I told my crew no permanent damage. The old bitch was a mistake. Word was to bruise 'em some and get them to drop the protest."

"Funny that." Ferguson shook his head. "You were all about stopping crime, and now you're the one going to jail."

***

Blue handed the phone to Molly.

"Sorry to take so long to get back to you. My guy had issues with the phone." Conrad's voice came through the phone.

"Besides it being dead?"

"There is hardware encryption on a second memory chip. That is no normal phone."

"Sorry, I forgot to mention it." Molly scratched Harley behind the ears and the dog flopped her head on Molly's lap.

"All that aside, the phone was tampered with. Essentially it turned on the location function to broadcast full time."

"So someone would know where I was and would be able to send people after me?"

"That would be the idea. The security features of the phone detected the issue when you tried to boot it and it shut down." Conrad sighed. "The people who gave you the phone could probably tell you how to reboot it, but unless you need something on the phone, it might be easier to get a new phone. There's always a chance it won't boot right, and you'll be stuck again."

"I will get a new phone, but I'd like that one back. A friend gave it to me."

"I'll pry it away from my tech friend."

"Thanks."

"Any word from Sergeant Ferguson recently?"

"No, but I sent him a present." Molly filled Conrad in on the incident at the coffee shop.

"Sounds like a good person to have off the street. You still be careful; he may have friends."

"I will be careful, but I don't want to end up afraid to go outside."

"Maybe I'll drop a word to Sergeant Ferguson about the tampering. He'll probably want his own people to look at it."

"If he wants it, let him have it, but I still want it back."

"As evidence, it could take a while."

"I can wait," Molly played with Harley's ears' "if it will get him off my back."

"Be safe." Conrad hung up and Molly handed the phone back to Blue.

"What did I do to anger someone so much they would do all this to get at me?"

"Who knows?" Blue shrugged. "I'm off to bed."

"Good plan. Tomorrow will be busy. I'm going to try to visit Agatha tomorrow, so I'll be late getting to the Café. Tell Tad not to worry."

"Sure thing."

# Chapter 17
**Wednesday, October 13**

Molly finished her coffee and sighed. She'd better walk Harley and get on her way to visit Agatha.

"Harley, walk."

The dog brought her leash over and sat as Molly clipped her on. They walked down the three flights of stairs to go out the door. The breeze was chilly, but for some reason, it didn't feel as cold here as it did downtown. They went over to Nelson Avenue, then down to Schubert. The water had risen a bit so there wasn't much beach for Harley to run on, but the trees blocked some of the wind.

Molly considered the questions she wanted to ask Agatha and what she'd do if her boss couldn't answer them. She also hadn't heard from the City about being part of the mayoral candidates' debate. Would they even let her in?

The whole thing with Cam's murder made no sense either. She didn't like him but only wanted him to leave her alone. That someone killed him was horrific, but that they'd tried to frame Molly? Who hated her that much? It was before the protests so it couldn't be the people like that man in the coffee shop.

Harley's whine brought her out of her thoughts. A scan of the area revealed no animals or people.

"Ready to go home, girl?" The temperature had to have dropped. Harley's fur was short, so she did get cold. Her missing leg had to bother her in this weather. Molly turned and headed back to the apartment. Harley's hackles were up, but Molly didn't see anyone. Even so, she quickened her steps, trusting the dog's instincts over her own. They arrived at the apartment building, and she unlocked the door and heaved a sigh. One of the reasons Blue liked the place was the halfway decent security.

Molly ran up the stairs with Harley in the lead and opened her door, slipped in, and leaned back, her heart racing like someone had been chasing her with a knife. Before she did anything else she made sure the door was properly closed and locked.

She made some tea and settled in to relax her nerves. Everything going on was playing with her mind. Nan had her creeped out with her tales of the street being in a bad mood. Spirits didn't inhabit the street; the pavement didn't care about bloodshed. She'd seen enough in her life. A shudder ran through her as the image of Cam's body flashed into her mind.

The warmth of the tea soothed her nerves, and she pulled her bag over and dug into the papers. The next bus wouldn't be for a while, and Molly liked getting to the stop just before the bus arrived.

Molly lost track of time working on answers to questions she hoped were, or weren't, asked at the debate. The knock on the door made her jump. She had her hand on the doorknob before she heard Harley's rumbling growl.

"Okay, girl, I won't open the door. Keep guard until they go away." Molly went back to the table but couldn't concentrate. How long would they wait out there? She wasn't expecting anyone from the building, and Ciara would have buzzed to get in.

"I'll just check the peephole," Molly said to the dog, but Harley's growl grew louder. "Okay, okay. I'll call Blue." But her phone was dead even if she'd had it. Maybe she could call him with the computer…

A bang came from the door, and the scream of wood echoed as the door wrenched open. Harley leaped forward, but the first person through the door tased the dog. She howled and twitched on the floor.

"Harley!" Molly screamed before a taser hit her, and she too dropped to the floor.

She fought to regain control of her twitching muscles as the men hoisted her up, stuffed a gag in her mouth, and carried her out of the apartment. One went ahead down the stairs and whistled before the others followed. They hauled her out the back door as she managed to kick with her legs. Molly fought with everything she had to not be thrown in the back of the van as a man in a mask, sunglasses, and a ball cap slapped the side of the van and hissed at them to hurry. The three men stuffed her through the door and clambered into the vehicle.

***

Mike polished his barber shop. He'd done all the work himself making it look like it had been there forever. He was a good haircutter, but a guy needed a gimmick to get ahead. The old school shop was popular enough to pay the rent on the storefront. Researching the changes on the street was fun.

He'd just waved goodbye to one of his better customers, a good tipper too, when a girl walked into the shop. She wore a loose flannel shirt and a ball cap along with her mask which had a picture of pursed lips on it. She had a backpack that looked stuffed to the limit. It had an 'Agatha for Mayor' button on it.

"Sorry, I don't do girl's cuts." Mike picked up his broom to sweep up.

"Just need to use the bathroom." The girl hopped from foot to foot, then bolted through the door into the back of the shop.

"Hey!" he shouted.

"Don't you ever clean in here?" The girl's complaint came out to him, and Mike rolled his eyes. She wasn't the first street person to use the washroom.

He finished sweeping and realized he hadn't heard from her, and she hadn't come back out. If she was robbing him, she'd find slim pickings back there. He kept his cash in his pocket.

*Maybe she's shooting up.*

Mike hated drugs. He'd been a slave to them for decades before he broke the chain. It left him with a disgust for people who did drugs.

*Not in my washroom.*

He put the broom in its corner and stomped into the back to bang on the washroom door.

"You'd better not be shooting up in there."

No answer, so he rattled the doorknob. "The lock doesn't work so I'm coming in on the count of three. One…two…three… Fine then, have it your way." He wrenched the door open and stepped into the tiny cubical expected to catch her with a needle in her arm.

She was standing flat against the wall all her clothes in place no needle in sight.

"Sorry."

"Just get –" His words were cut off by a knife stabbing into his throat. Blood flowed into his airway, making him choke.

"I'm not really sorry." The girl pulled the blade out and stabbed him again. "There's something satisfying about stabbing a man."

He tried to grab her and knocked her hat off, but she slashed her knife across his face. The stabs came quicker, and he couldn't breathe or move. The last thing he felt was something being put into his hand.

***

Ferguson held his phone to his ear with his shoulder while talking to Callister's lawyer about the girl's cellphone.

"What do you mean, tampered with?"

"Just like it sounds." The lawyer sounded as relaxed as one who gets paid $275 an hour. "Someone set the phone to be a tracking beacon."

"How do I know you didn't fiddle with the phone?"

"You don't, but we both know it is no longer admissible evidence."

"So why tell me?"

"I thought you might find it useful to know that someone was very interested in Molly's whereabouts leading up to the murder."

"Why would they care?"

"Maybe so they could be sure she'd be the one to find the body."

"Right. You read too many detective novels."

"Ferguson!" Hassim stuffed her phone in her pocket. "Sorry to interrupt. There's been another murder downtown. Guy wanting a haircut found the body."

"Damn." Ferguson followed her out to the car and got in the passenger seat as she sped off. "What do we know?"

"Not much." She pulled up in front of the barber shop. A cruiser sat out front, and the constable was moving people along with a glower. They put on boots and gloves and walked carefully through the immaculate shop. The door to the back was open. A pile of vomit showed where the person who called it in lost their lunch. Ferguson leaned in to look. It wasn't pleasant, blood had splashed all over the walls and the place stank of shit and guts.

"Stay here. I'm going to go check the back door." He left the shop and walked through the alley to where the back door swung open. A pile of bloody clothes lay in a pile. "Either they came prepared, or there's a naked perp running through the streets." Ferguson called to Hassim, "Send someone 'round back to watch the door. Tell the scene of crime people to call us with updates. I'm going to walk the alley; come watch my back."

Whoever killed the man inside the shop in the middle of the day wouldn't hold back against the police. Ferguson was all too aware that his ballistic vest wouldn't stop a hard blow with a knife.

***

Harley shook off the taser bolt. She'd been hit with them before. Her person was in trouble. Harley could smell the fear.

Molly had told her to guard, and she would find her person and make them safe. The dog dashed through the door following her person's scent. Down the stairs to a closed door. She knew this kind and barely slowed as she hit the crash bar. The door flung open and banged against the wall. A van stood outside with a man leaning out a window.

"Shit!" He yelled and floored the van out onto the street, then squealed through a left turn onto Fortune. Harley ran flat out after the van. Brakes screeched and people screamed. The van wove through traffic, but the road was full of cars.

Harley's top speed over a short distance reached seventy kilometres an hour. In the traffic, the van could only manage sixty. Harley caught up as the van swerved left to leave Fortune. Harley had been trained for this. She launched her hundred and ninety pounds through the window slamming into the driver. The driver screamed something, but Harley didn't have time for him. She spun and lunged into the back. One of the men had a taser, but Harley bit his arm and shook. Bones cracked and the man shrieked. The dog was already attacking the next man who tried to swing a crowbar at her. A crunch and he was down. The van swerved wildly as cars honked

"Call it off!" The last man hid behind Molly. She readied herself to launch but the van stopped with a crash and Harley flew to slam into the windshield. Molly hit her as the man who had held her smashed into the back of the passenger seat.

Harley hurt everywhere, but Molly was lying on the floor of the van and still needed guarding. The dog crouched beside her person and growled. None of the men did anything but moan, but Harley would guard until her person released her.

***

"Miss." A voice penetrated the fog in Molly's head. "Miss, you have to call the dog off. We can't help anyone until you call off the dog."

Molly pulled herself upright.

"It's okay, Harley. Release." Harley slumped against her and whined. The paramedics clambered in to assess and help the men out of the van.

"My dog needs a vet," Molly shouted.

"Sorry, we can't do dogs."

The men were groaning as the paramedics wrapped their wounds.

"They tried to kidnap me," Molly called out. She moved experimentally. Nothing seemed to be broken. Harley whined again and licked her hand.

"Good dog." The whining lessened, then stopped. Molly buried her face in Harley's fur as agonizing sobs wrenched out of her.

"We need to check you out." A paramedic crawled over to Molly and went through her assessment.

"Shaken up, but I don't think anything is broken, but you might be bleeding internally. We need to get you to the hospital.

"At least put a blanket over her."

The paramedic came back with a blanket and laid it over the dog. "I will tell them to take proper care of her."

As they helped her out of the van, she saw it had hit a tree. Steam rose from the busted radiator. Molly was strapped onto a stretcher and lifted into an ambulance.

The wail of the siren pulled at Molly's heart. Tears ran from her eyes into her ears. She couldn't move to wipe them away, so let them flow.

# Chapter 18

Ferguson looked around in frustration. The perp had just vanished like a ghost. He was on the phone with the SOC team, but they couldn't tell him anything yet and were annoyed that he'd called so soon.

Hassim's phone rang. She answered, then her mouth dropped open.

"What is going on with this city?" Hassim put her phone away. "Murder in the middle of the morning. Now an attempted kidnapping, stopped, according to witnesses, by a big black dog that ran down the van and steered it into a tree."

"You're joking." Ferguson glared at her.

"No joke, they just hauled the survivors up to the hospital."

"Survivors?"

"The driver had a crushed chest, another a broken neck. Report is the dog died too."

"We'd better hoof it back to the car and get up to the hospital."

They arrived in emergency and were led to where two men were being treated for dog bites and broken bones. A stony-faced constable stood in the room.

"So there was a dog," Hassim said.

"I thought it was going to rip out my throat," one man groaned. "My arm will never be the same."

"Not if you don't sit still. We'll send you for x-rays now that the bleeding has stopped," the nurse said.

"Never should have listened to that bitch."

"Which one?" Ferguson pulled out his notebook.

"The one on the phone, wanted this chick picked up. We fucking tased the dog, and it still ran us down."

"My heart bleeds for you." Ferguson looked at the man over his notebook. "Does the bitch have a name?"

"Calls herself Molly, but I never met her. Zack and Hank did all the talking to her. Heard you busted Hank and the dog did for Zack."

"Hassim, see if you can get anything from these two." Ferguson snapped his notebook shut. "I'm going to find the victim and see if they can make a statement." He found a nurse who took him to a room with a woman curled up on the bed.

"They did a CAT scan. There is no internal bleeding, but she's pretty shook up." The nurse put a hand on the woman's shoulder. "There's a police officer here to talk to you."

"All right." The woman sat up. "Oh great, just what I needed to complete my day."

"My thoughts exactly." Ferguson pulled out a notebook and pencil.

"Do I need a lawyer?" Callister asked.

"Don't think being a victim of an attempted kidnapping is a crime, but who knows?"

"What do you want?"

"Tell me what happened, in your own words."

"Three guys busted into my apartment. They tased my dog and me. I thought I was a goner, couldn't move and Harley…" she choked up. "Harley couldn't protect me. They carried me downstairs and put me in a van, then took off. The one guy was on about how they were going to mess me up and enjoy it. Creep. Then Harley came through the passenger window and tore into the guys in the van."

"I saw some of her work," Ferguson said.

"The van hit a something, and everything flew about. Harley hit the windshield and took the force when I hit, or I would have gone through the glass. Next thing I remember is the paramedic telling me to call off the dog. She was still guarding me."

"I heard the dog didn't make it. I'm sorry."

Molly choked up again. "She saved my life more than once."

"You weren't anywhere near the Café today?"

"No. I was going to visit Agatha, but they told me I wasn't allowed. I was going to go to the Café later."

"Okay, that will do for now. I'll get something more formal when you're up to it."

Ferguson went to find Hassim.

"Hank mentioned a woman; so did the clowns involved in the kidnapping," Hassim said as they left the hospital.

"Maybe have another talk with Hank, if we can find him," Ferguson said. "Callister wasn't murdering the barber if she was across town getting kidnapped."

"And if she was faking the abduction, it would have been something less violent." Hassim opened the cruiser door. "That dog had to be a police dog or some military animal. No one in their right mind would fake violence around it."

"The idiots probably saw the dog and figured they could handle it with the taser." Ferguson buckled in and reached for the radio. "I'll put out a bulletin on Hank and see where that takes us." It wasn't far to Battle Street Station.

He sat at his desk and ran through the evidence. He didn't like the conclusion. Someone was gunning for Callister and didn't much care about collateral damage. This wasn't over.

***

Molly held onto Blue for a long time when he showed up at the hospital.

"Poor Harley." Molly sniffled.

"Yeah." Blue squeezed her, then stepped back. "I'll have to get onto the insurance about the door, then get it repaired. Do you want to come to the apartment, or should I drop you at the Café?"

"Café, I don't want to go home to an empty apartment."

They took the bus down to Victoria and Molly limped into the Café.

"Good God," Erica said. "What happened?"

"I don't want to talk about it." Molly went to her table and realized all her notes were at the apartment. The idea of going and getting them seemed too heartbreaking. Instead, she put her head on the table and concentrated on not crying.

Tad put a cup of coffee on the table by Molly's elbow and went back to the kitchen. She drank some coffee and started feeling more human. Anger rose in place of the sadness.

*How dare they!*

Tad sat across from her and put another cup of coffee beside her.

"I have a few minutes if you need to talk."

"What are you making today?"

"Shepherd's Pie"

"That sounds good." Molly gave up on normal and stared into her cup. "Some people tried to snatch me and killed my dog."

"You sound more upset about the dog."

"I am. If they hadn't been so stupid, Harley would be alive."

"What was Harley like?"

"She only had three legs because she took a bullet for Blue, but it never slowed her down. Harley could lie beside me, and all my anxieties would disappear. People were scared of her because she was big and black, but she wouldn't hurt anyone unless they attacked me or Blue."

By the time she finished talking about Harley, the grief had begun to ease its clutch on her heart. It had been more than a few minutes, but Tad didn't fidget. He squeezed her hand, then went back into the kitchen.

She didn't know anyone who talked less than Tad, but he was a good listener. At least she assumed he was listening.

It was sit in the corner and feel sorry for herself, or get to work. She wandered through the room talking to people. Everyone asked after Agatha, who was a hero for getting the Café opened again. Molly invited all of them to come to the debate the next evening.

192

At closing time, Tad walked Molly to the bus stop and waited with her. As she rode the bus, she considered who knew where she lived. Someone had to be watching her. Those times Harley growled weren't a bear or another dog.

She'd had to fill out her mailing and home address on the forms for financial officer. Only Agatha had seen those papers, but they'd sat on the desk for a day. Maybe someone came in and looked at them?

Someone who had reason to hate her.

Molly shook her head. She had people after her before, but there wasn't the feeling of raw hate. She already found it hard enough to go out, this would only make it worse. *I won't become a recluse.* But now she didn't have Harley to guard her on her walks.

Her heart raced as the bus pulled up to her stop. Would someone be waiting for her? A figure stood in the gloom. It wore the scarf she'd knit for Blue ages ago. She barely waited for the bus to stop before she jumped off and hugged Blue.

"Come on, it's chilly out here." Blue headed for the apartment. "The superintendent was furious. He talked a lot in Russian, I think he was cursing. But then he got people over and had the door fixed within a couple hours."

"Maybe it was the assault on his building that made him made so angry."

"Perhaps."

A sign on the door read. 'Do Not Allow Anyone in the Building If You Don't Know Them.'

They climbed the stairs and Blue unlocked the door and let her into the apartment. "New door. New lock. New keys."

The place felt as empty as Molly had feared, the dog's bed an immediate reminder of her loss.

"I'll make supper." Molly opened the fridge trying to decide what to cook. Blue turned on the tv.

"…in a daring daylight abduction attempt two of the perpetrators were killed and two others mauled by a dog…"

Molly slammed the fridge shut and swore. "It wasn't daring, it was fucking stupid, and if Harley had mauled them, there would have been four dead."

"It's just the news." Blue switched the tv off.

"Shit." Molly tried to concentrate on supper, but the line from the newscast ran through her head like a spike. She began a kata in the living room focusing on nothing but her breathing. It didn't stop the heartache, but it gave her something to do instead of dropping to the floor and wailing. It had been too long since she had properly practiced, not since starting school in September.

When she stopped, sweaty and shaking, Blue had supper almost ready.

194

"I'm going to have a shower." Molly dragged herself to the shower. Under the flowing water, she let the tears run. She stayed until her fingers turned to prunes. Not feeling like getting properly dressed, she put on her pajamas and bathrobe.

"Molly." Ciara jumped up to run and hug her tightly.

"Ouch." Molly's ribs complained.

"Sorry." Ciara looked on the edge of tears.

"It's okay." Molly wrapped the younger girl in her arms and held her without moving. Her ribs hurt, bruises ached, and the loss of Harley was a black hole in her heart. But for this moment being held by Ciara, Molly stopped feeling like she was falling apart.

***

Ferguson stood in the morgue as the coroner conducted the autopsy on Mike duBois.

"See here," she pointed to the wound in the throat. "This was the killing blow. He didn't die right away, but his life was measured in minutes, if that. The other wounds are window dressing. The killer hit him hard, then took their time to make it look like a frantic attack."

"It wasn't a spur of the moment thing then." Ferguson's mind was drawn to a few days ago when it was Robinson's corpse on the table. "Are there any hesitation cuts?"

"Interesting question. I can't say for sure until I've checked the whole body, but each strike appears precise and on target. Did you find a weapon?"

"Not yet."

"You won't then." The coroner adjusted the plastic mask protecting her face with the back of her hand.

"What makes you say that?"

"From what I've been told about the crime scene, it was meticulously planned. The killer probably wore two layers of clothing so they could shed one and emerge a different person. If she wanted you to find the weapon, you would have."

"You're saying we're dealing with an evil genius?" Ferguson raised an eyebrow.

"No, but the killer sees themselves as a master manipulator, pulling the strings to move the police." The coroner peered at a wound.

"Someone who could kill with a single stab to the heart then?" Ferguson asked

"I would say so."

"Damn, and she set us on Callister like dogs on a rabbit."

"Don't feel too bad. It is hard to see clearly when the facts are obscured." The coroner looked up for a second before returning to work.

They finished up the autopsy, and Ferguson went to find Hassim.

"Join me after shift for a drink. I owe you a beer."

"Just let me give Lia a call. I'm going to order the most expensive fancy, schmancy beer they have."

"As long as I don't have to drink it."

***

"So, to what do I owe this marvelous beverage?" Hassim sipped at the amber ale.

"You stopped me from doing something stupid." Ferguson took a pull of his Molson's. "I was out of line with Callister."

"It's what partners are for." Hassim grinned over her glass.

"Back to the evidence," Ferguson said. "What do we have?"

"Murder, someone expert with a knife. If it hadn't been for the jacket and the timing, we would have hardly looked at Callister. The killer wanted us distracted."

"From what?" Ferguson took another swallow. "If Callister was out of the picture, what would we have done different?"

"Focus on family and friends first. It seems too neat to be random."

"What about the two in Vancouver?"

"If you were a hooker and had to kill a man a lot bigger than you, wouldn't you want to slow them down? Hard to fight with one's pants around the ankles." Hassim frowned. "Manipulate your victim into a weak place, then strike."

"Right. Tomorrow let's take another look at Robinson's background." Ferguson finished his beer. "You talk to the girlfriend. I'll get his father.

***

## Thursday, October 14

"Just a few more questions." Hassim sat across from Carlotta in the fancy house up in Aberdeen.

"Fine, but make it quick, I have to leave to catch a flight in an hour."

"Where are you going?"

"School. I'm going to transfer to a fine arts school in New York."

"Rather sudden, isn't it?"

"Not really. I applied last spring. I'll start in January." Carlotta tapped her fingers on the table. "Look, let me be straight here. I played the tragic girlfriend, but I was going to dump him. He couldn't stop screwing around. He thought I didn't know, but he'd asked me out of the blue in the spring what I'd look like as a blonde."

"Right. Just for the record where were you the night of September 27."

"I was here playing princess for my father's business contacts. Like his Rolls, he likes to dangle me in front of others."

"Okay, good luck in New York."

"You aren't going to tell me not to leave town?" Carlotta had already got up and started for the door.

"You don't look like you'd be that good with a knife." Hassim smiled and handed Carlotta a card. "If you think of anything else we should know, send me an email."

"Of course." She immediately dropped it on a table in the entry hall.

***

Ferguson met Mr. Robinson in his study. He had a clear view of the large 'John Brown for Mayor' sign on the lawn.

"I don't have a lot of time, Sergeant."

"Just a few follow-up questions. Cameron had a girlfriend, correct?" Ferguson had his pad and pen ready.

"Yes, an artist, Carlotta."

"How was their relationship?"

"Fine, they were to be married after graduation. She was very broken up about Cameron's death." Mr. Robinson shook his head sadly.

"From all accounts, Cameron had a thing for Molly Callister."

Mr. Robinson winced slightly. "He simply wanted to apologize for a foolish remark. She made it into an unnecessary fuss."

"Are there any other women Cameron found it necessary to apologize to?"

Mr. Robinson looked at his watch.

"I've given you all the time I can, Sergeant. I will see you out."

***

"By the way he gave me the bum's rush, I suspect he knew about his son's side interests." Ferguson bit into his sandwich from the Subway on Victoria Street.

"Carlotta had no illusions about Robinson but didn't care enough to kill him. I think any man she has will play second fiddle to her art." Hassim leaned back.

"So, we have mystery woman on the side, who may or may not have been jealous of the undue attention Callister got from him."

"Why the second killing and the attempted abduction?" Hassim shook her head and then dug into her salad.

"Control." Ferguson snapped his fingers. "Doc said the perp was a master manipulator, manipulators have to be pulling strings. I'll bet the clowns were supposed to deliver Callister to the manipulator so they could revel in their brilliance."

"The second killing still isn't needed."

"If Callister vanished, wouldn't we suspect her more and not look at other possibilities?"

"It's still a stretch," Hassim said doubtfully.

"Of course, it is. If they'd left well enough alone after murder number one, we might never have solved it. All the evidence was circumstantial and pointed in the wrong direction. But they couldn't stop and so things got out of control."

"What's next? Blonde hardly narrows the field."

"We go to a debate and watch for someone with a hate-on for Callister."

# Chapter 19

The mayor's office phoned in mid-afternoon to tell Molly they were going to allow her to speak. She sat down to breathe for a minute, then called Ciara on her computer to tell her the debate was on. Ciara would hand out leaflets and monitor the audience the same way Molly had.

Molly dressed in pants and a suit jacket she'd bought at a thrift shop and gathered her notes. She and Blue walked out to wait for the bus. Every white van made her shake, and there were a lot of white vans. By the time she got on the bus, Molly was a nervous wreck.

"I guess that is one way to get rid of pre-speech nerves." Molly clutched her bag. "Have something else give you an anxiety attack."

"You'll be all right. Just pretend you are arguing with me, and you'll be fine."

"I know, but I can't help thinking I'm in over my head."

"And if you are, you'll learn how to swim."

"I'm still not much of a swimmer." Molly laughed, then winced.

The bus left them off at First and Seymour and they walked down to the Sandman where the debate was being hosted.

Molly had to weave her way through the crowd to get to a woman with a clipboard.

"I'm Molly Callister. I'm speaking for Agatha Howard."

"So I was told." The woman didn't look pleased. "Follow me and I will take you to the waiting room. Try not to get into any arguments. Save them for the debate."

Molly didn't ask if she'd warned the other candidates the same way.

The other candidates had already arrived, and most were huddling with assistants. Molly was the only one alone. She sat in a corner and breathed slowly, trying to hold her bag rather than clutch it like a teddy bear.

"Excuse me, miss. Pick a ball from the bag." A young man held a black velvet bag.

"She should just take what is left." John Brown looked daggers at Molly.

"You will have to take that up with the mayor. I'm just doing my job."

Molly picked the number one position. *Just like school, but I think I got a decent mark on that.*

The young man made a note on the clipboard and moved on.

"Ten minutes," the woman with the clipboard told them and picked up the list from the young man.

The mayor came in five minutes before the debate was to start.

"Let's have a good debate." He left before John Brown and another candidate could catch him.

"You'll want to watch and learn," one of the candidates said to Molly. "He's a master of avoidance. Paul Admanson." He offered a fist bump. "Last poll had you ahead of me. I plan to catch up to you tonight."

"Good luck." Molly grinned and Paul laughed.

They filed out to the platform and sat in the chair with their name. Molly almost missed hers as it said *Molly Callister*, not *Agatha Howard*. Fortunately, John Brown was sitting two people over.

"Good evening." The mayor stepped up to the mic. "Welcome to the mayoral candidates' debate." The conference room was full, with people standing around the walls.

"Objection. One of the speakers isn't a candidate. She's a prostitute and drug addict." John Brown stood up.

"This isn't a courtroom. You can object all you want, but it won't change a thing. We've been over this. You don't like it; you know where the door is."

"I have it on good authority, Agatha Howard is in a vegetative state and should be removed from the ballot."

"Your good authority is bupkis. I spoke with Ms. Howard today." The mayor frowned. "There will be no third warning, Mr. Brown. Sit down and wait your turn to speak."

John Brown's mouth opened and closed a few times before he sat and glared at Molly. She ignored him, concentrating on convincing her legs to be ready to move when her turn came.

"Our first speaker is Molly Callister, speaking on behalf of Ag—"

"Boo!" Came from several places in the audience. "Hooker, junkie."

"SILENCE!" The mayor boomed, and Molly had to stop her hands from covering her ears. "This is equivalent to a meeting of Council and disruption will not be tolerated. Be quiet or leave."

"You can't make me."

"I can." An RCMP officer in full dress red serge stepped forward.

"Try and find me."

"He's over here, officer." Someone raised a hand.

"One's over here too."

Several other people raised their hands.

Two other officers in red stepped out from the back corners.

The room went quiet.

"I think I must explain the rules. There will be no interruptions of a candidate's speech, from the floor or from other candidates. I will not issue another warning. During question time you may ask *questions.*" The mayor laid on the emphasis. "Personally, I am looking forward to all the speeches. As I was saying, Molly is speaking on behalf of Agatha Howard who was injured in an unfortunate altercation. The police continue to investigate and have three of the hoodlums in custody.

"Agatha is the only candidate to have served as mayor, serving a term in Spruce Bay. She ran a thrift shop and is presently living with a friend. She had several interesting things to say at the last debate. Molly is here to build on that foundation. Molly Callister." The mayor clapped and a surprising number of the audience did as well.

"Good evening, I bring greetings from Agatha Howard. I may be speaking, but the principles and ideas come from her notes." The shakiness left her knees.

"People have called me a prostitute and a junkie. So what? It is nothing but the truth from a few years back. Thanks to good friends, I got off the street where I'd been forced to sell myself since I was fifteen. I attend NA meetings and have my four years sober pin.

Agatha is homeless. That doesn't make her less worthy of your attention or your vote.

The heat in Molly's gut carried her on.

"Agatha mentioned several ways of increasing property tax revenue without increasing taxes, by encouraging higher-density buildings, especially downtown, and infilling spaces with multi-level properties that will pay much more per square foot than the box stores on the edge of town."

"Such building will also help to continue the rejuvenation of the downtown." She spoke from the notes but putting them in her own words with her own passion.

"Policing is the single greatest expense the city has. It is a tough job and made tougher by the fact that police are required to be social workers, mediators, and more on top of their job of keeping the peace. Moving some of those tasks to people trained specifically for the work will free up police time to handle crimes and deal with criminals. Increased social services will remove the element of poverty which has a direct relationship to crime, poor health and more."

"In conclusion, I urge you to think out of the box and consider voting for Agatha Howard."

The applause wasn't thunderous, but it was more than polite. Some people in the crowd waved. 'Agatha for Mayor' posters, and Erica gave her a thumbs up. Ciara beamed from ear to ear. Molly took her seat.

Paul Admanson was the next speaker.

"That, folks, is why Agatha is running third in the polls." Paul nodded in Molly's direction. "I could say I would implement many of those ideas and sit down, but what politician can resist the chance to speak? I have a few notions of my own. One is to add an absentee landlord tax to encourage local people to purchase and own both business and residential properties…"

John Brown was next, and he stalked up to the mic.

"What kind of city are we if we encourage criminals, even reformed criminals to be our leaders…" He ranted for most of his allotted time, only squeezing in a few comments about increasing policing and bylaws enforcement in the last minutes. He stomped back to his seat with another glare at Molly.

The next speaker did her bit and after the final speaker, the mayor declared they would have a ten-minute break before the question period.

***

Ferguson wandered the room. He was there as an extra layer of security should it be needed. He and six other officers were in plain clothes for the event. He'd identified the speaker daring the mayor to remove him as an associate of Hank's. He'd already detailed a couple of constables to pick him up for questioning.

There were a lot of people looking angrily in Molly's direction, but none of them were blonde girls of an age to be friends with Cameron Robinson. He expected the question period to be considerably rowdier and hoped he didn't get distracted from what was, for him, the primary purpose of the evening – to scout out people who looked like a real threat to Callister.

She impressed him with her speech; radical enough to suit Agatha Howard, who by all accounts was a firecracker at her first appearance, and who'd rallied the pro-Café forces, refusing to be intimidated by the counter-protesters, but with enough bones thrown to the status quo people. He was considering voting for Agatha, but the potential cuts in the police budget worried him.

The speakers mostly went to mingle with the crowd, but John Brown stayed at his seat and a young woman brought him water and looked to be encouraging him. Molly wandered through the crowd talking to people, especially a young First Nations girl who had handfuls of leaflets.

A few people looked to be starting trouble, but Callister's father might have been a cop working a security detail and cut them off. Blue didn't need to say much to convince the would-be troublemakers to back off. Ferguson was impressed.

"Think that Blue is an ex-cop?" He asked Hassim

"I'd give you at least even odds, even if I didn't already know he is. It was buried in one of the earlier articles following the explosion that killed a bunch of dealers."

"Right, I think we can relax a little with him watching Callister's back." He glanced to the front to catch the young woman who'd brought the water to John Brown standing behind him. Her hands were white on the chair, and if looks could kill, Callister would be dead several times over.

"Find out who that young woman behind John Brown is." Ferguson nodded toward the girl.

The lights flickered, and the crowd moved back to their seats except for a few who pre-emptively staked their claim on the question mics. He spotted a couple of the troublemakers and winced. They wouldn't be kind to Callister, but then politics was a blood sport.

They started the questions with the mayor moderating. The first question started the trouble.

"A question for Ms. Callister. Are you in favour of legalizing prostitution?"

A woman handed Callister a mic.

"It depends on what you mean by prostitution. If you are talking about walking the street, then no, there is too much opportunity for pimps to move in and make young men or women virtual slaves. If you are talking about a woman choosing to sell her services, then perhaps. It would need to be licensed and require regular health checks."

The man's face was a study in conflict. He clearly wanted to ask another question, but the mayor frowned at him from the podium. Common sense won a brief victory. The next questioner added to the question.

"Molly, how much does a prostitute make? Shouldn't they be taxed?"

"I made nothing from being a prostitute for six years. I can't tell you what the pimps made. If you want to learn more about the sex trade, I can recommend some good books."

The man fled from the mic.

"How can you talk about decreasing the police budget when crime in Kamloops is at an all-time high?" A woman frowned at Molly.

This time the mic was handed to another candidate first who assured the woman he had no intention of decreasing the budget.

Molly was the last to speak to the question. "Crime has grown in proportion to the police budget. Maybe addressing the root causes of crime will be more effective. Some jurisdictions have hired social workers to respond to mental health and welfare checks with some success."

"If you were a social worker, would you want to go on a call that makes police officers nervous?" The woman's frown deepened.

"I'm a social work student, and yes, if the job was offered, I'd be first in line to apply."

"A question for John Brown: why do you think the crime rate has increased?"

"We are too soft on criminals. If they want homes, well, put them in prison! It is time to stop coddling people who are too lazy to get their life in order."

Molly put a hand up. "If I may ask Mr. Brown a question."

*This should be interesting.*

"If you had no money, no job, no home, no transportation and, if you were lucky, two sets of clothes, how would you go about putting your life in order?"

"If you can't get your life in order, you deserve to go to prison for your crimes."

"Assuming someone has committed a crime and is sent to prison," Molly responded. "It costs between fifty and eighty thousand dollars a year to house them. For that money, we could pay for an apartment, social workers for support and free access to the bus system and still save at least twenty thousand a year."

People in the audience started yelling at Molly, then others yelled at the people in the crowd. A fight broke out, and Ferguson decided it was time to step in before it became a riot.

"I am a police officer, and there are other police officers in plain clothes through the crowd." He used his 'stop, I'm a police officer' voice. "I think in the interests of public safety, this meeting should be ended."

The mayor glared at him but went to the mic and declared the meeting adjourned. The crowd filed out, looking about to see who the police among them were.

"Thank you, officer." The mayor came over to talk to Ferguson. He still didn't look happy, but except for a bit of shouting outside, the room was quiet.

John Brown also came over.

"A demonstration of what I have said. We need a strong police presence to maintain the peace."

"By the way," Ferguson asked, trying to look pleased with Brown's praise. "Who was the young woman who brought you water?

"That was my daughter, Carolyn Mason. You won't see her making a spectacle of herself in public." Brown looked around for Callister, but she'd already left, Ferguson hoped, by a side entrance.

"Thank you for your time." Ferguson made his escape and found Hassim outside talking to three dejected-looking young men.

"They were just leaving, weren't you?" She fixed them with a steady gaze.

"Yes, officer." They almost ran off.

"Idiots. They were looking for Molly to ask her on a date."

"Blue is with her. He'll watch her back. Get two of the cruisers to push their flashers on. Remind people we're here."

***

Molly followed Blue, hanging on to Ciara's hand.

"Figured you'd go out the side." Erica waved. "I brought a few peacekeepers to get you home safe. One of them is trying to flag down a taxi."

"Thanks, Erica." Blue walked casually alongside her. "Looks like they've corralled our ride home."

Blue made sure Molly and Ciara were secured in the cab before climbing into the passenger seat.

214

"North Shore." Blue waved a couple of twenties. The driver crawled through the dispersing crowd. He made better time once he was on Victoria Street West.

Once at home, Molly flopped on the couch and looked for Harley. The absence was an ache in her heart, but she had Blue and Ciara.

"What did you think, Ciara?"

"You were awesome!"

They talked until Ciara's eyes closed, and she fell asleep on the couch. Molly put a blanket over her and went to bed. It wasn't the first time the girl had slept over, and her presence made the apartment less empty.

Molly had a dream that Harley stood between her and someone in the shadows, but oddly familiar.

*Thanks, Harley, I'll pay attention.*

# Chapter 20

**Friday, October 15**

After breakfast, Hanna picked up Ciara while Blue took the bus to the Café and Molly headed for the university. She did the rounds of her professors, apologizing for her absence the past week and getting caught up on what assignments she needed to complete.

The weather had changed from overcast and cold to sunny and crisp. Her ribs didn't hurt too badly; the bright day helped her feel less gloomy. She'd only missed a week, but it felt like a lot longer. It wouldn't be too hard to do the readings and the few assignments.

Carolyn approached Molly while she walked to her next appointment. "What have you been up to?"

"Election stuff, mostly."

"My father told me to drop that and concentrate on school, but you didn't miss much. Social work history is as boring as ever. If you haven't, you'll want to check in with Professor Huston."

"I have an appointment in half an hour." Molly shrugged and winced slightly.

"Ribs still hurt?"

"Some," Molly said. "But I'm lucky it was a bat, not a crowbar."

"Yes indeed." Carolyn frowned. "How about we get together tomorrow and watch the election results?"

"I'm planning on watching it from the Café, sorry."

"Going to hang out with your boyfriend?" Carolyn's voice had a snide twist to it.

"What?" Molly stared at Carolyn. "I don't have a boyfriend."

"Oh, my mistake." Carolyn reddened. "I have to be on my way. Clinical is in a few minutes. Maybe we can meet up after."

"I'm headed down to the Café after my appointment with Professor Huston."

"Fine, then. See you next week." Carolyn walked away briskly.

Molly headed for her appointment with Professor Huston.

"I'm not sure what to do with you," he said. "I know you've been working hard, but it is hardly social work."

"Isn't community social work about advocacy and policy? I've been working harder on them than on any of my other course assignments." She kept the edge of panic out of her voice

"Perhaps." Professor Huston pulled on his beard. "How about you hand in a paper on what you've learned, and I'll go from there. It is too late for a different placement."

"I could work at the Loop or the Café," Molly offered, "and continue to learn about policy."

"I think I could allow you to finish up your hours at the Café. I'll be waiting with interest for your paper."

Molly took the bus down to the Café and entered to applause and cheers.

"You showed 'em," Erica said. "I'd vote for you."

"You can't vote for me; I'm not running." Molly laughed. "Vote for Agatha."

"You should run."

"Not me." Molly put her hands up. "I've had enough of politics. Where's Blue?"

"He had a meeting at the Loop. We're going to watch your speech again." Erica started up the video of the All-Candidates Meeting.

Molly cringed at hearing her voice on video, but the others didn't seem to notice anything strange. *Do I always sound like that?* They stopped the video occasionally to make comments or ask questions.

"Stop!" Molly leaned closer to the screen. "Carolyn was there. I'm sure that was her, but why didn't she say anything to me? I just saw her this morning."

"Maybe she forgot?" Erica shrugged.

"The police had to shut it down because it was turning into a riot. How could she forget that?"

"I guess."

Molly leaned back as they continued the video. Erica fast-forwarded through the break.

"Wait, back up a bit."

There was Carolyn bringing John Brown a glass of water. Molly searched her memory for Carolyn's last name, but it wasn't Brown, she was sure of that. As it rolled forward, they stopped again. Carolyn was staring at the crowd with an expression of loathing, as if she'd bitten into something rotten.

"Maybe that's your answer," Erica said. "She was working for the enemy."

"Perhaps." Molly's head ached. "Or she didn't want to be there. Her father told her to stay away from politics."

"Then why be there at all? There is something strange about that girl." Erica stared at the frozen picture on the screen.

"She thought I had a boyfriend," Molly said. "Why was that?"

"Maybe she saw you and Tad coming back from the coffee shop and made assumptions."

"Why would she be on the street? There was hardly anyone about." Molly's headache grew worse.

"What if she knew the guy who tried to punch me." Tad's voice made Molly start. She didn't know he'd come out of the kitchen. "He might assume I was your boyfriend."

"But he sounded like one of the guys who attacked us. Would Carolyn have anything to do with him?

"She was bringing water to John Brown," Erica said. "She was part of your campaign, wasn't she?"

"At the start, yeah, but most of the students gave up after a day or two. I thought she was just one of them." Molly rubbed her head. "She was in my class with Cameron, the guy who was harassing me."

"What of it?" Tad asked.

"The police questioned me about it. They found my jacket with him when he was murdered. Somebody was tracking my phone."

"That's some serious shit." Erica sat down. "Maybe you need a bodyguard, like in the movies."

"I don't know." Molly shook her head. "I need to talk to Blue."

"He'll be back soon," Tad said. "Maybe give me a hand in the kitchen until he gets back."

"Okay."

Tad wasn't much more talkative in the kitchen than anywhere else, but Molly found the rhythm of chopping soothing.

***

"So where are we?" Ferguson paced by his desk. Hassim leaned back in her chair and watched him.

"Not much of anywhere," Hassim said. "Sit down, you're making me dizzy."

Ferguson ignored her.

"Look, we have even less evidence of Mason's involvement than we had of Callister's" Hassim closed her eyes. "She has opportunity, unless we find she has an alibi. We don't know if she even owns a knife, never mind can kill with one. What would her motive be?"

"Don't know."

Ferguson dropped into his chair, making it creak. "I've got a bad feeling about this."

"Really?" Hassim sat up.

"If someone is trying to manipulate events, they aren't done. Unless they give up and go home, something else will happen. It will involve Callister."

"What makes you think that?"

"Everything else has centred around her." Ferguson's phone rang. "Ferguson… what? We'll be right down." He looked at Hassim with a triumphant grin on his face. "SOC has a gift for us."

Down in the lab, Ferguson looked around and wished, like he did every time, that they had a lab like the ones on TV. It struck him as utilitarian. It lacked the countless specialized pieces of equipment they had on TV

"First, the button." The scene of crime tech held it up, protected in an evidence bag. "We found a print, and no, it doesn't match Callister's. It isn't good enough for court, but there's a seventy-five percent match to the one etched on the knife blade. It is a left thumbprint and etched into the metal the same way as the knife. That suggests a very similar acidic sweat if they are from two different people. That is part one. The other is this." The tech held up another bag with a single hair in it, dyed red with blood.

"A hair? The victim was a barber."

"Yes, and we found a lot of hair on his clothes, but all of it cut and short. This one is shed and long, probably female. Witnesses placed a street kid on the scene, probably a girl. If you find the girl, we can match DNA and place her on the scene."

"The defence would tear it apart, one hair in a barbershop."

The tech looked affronted. "It was found on top of fresh blood. It was shed after the murder." They passed over a photograph.

"Our killer was possibly a blonde and possibly connected to the first murder." Ferguson frowned. "But is that enough to bring Mason in?"

"Probably not, but does she know that?" Hassim said. "All we need now is to find her."

"We should talk to Callister. Maybe she knows our mystery blonde."

"What we're going to ask 'Hey, do you know a blonde named Mason who might be killing people?'"

"I have work to do. Could you continue your discussion elsewhere?" The SOC tech glared at them.

***

Carolyn wanted to scream, but then Papa would come, and she'd have to explain. If he found out, she'd have to leave.

Why should Molly be so happy and confident? Why didn't she have to follow the rules? Carolyn thumped her bed. Papa had been clear: she could stay as long as she obeyed the rules, and the first rule was not to talk about her past. She hadn't meant to, but Molly's presentation was like a knife to the heart. Carolyn couldn't stop herself. Now she had to clean up her mess.

Papa was already furious about the debate and how that hussy had dared argue with him. Carolyn had caught the brunt of his anger when they'd got home. He'd lectured her on how a young woman should act until it was late, then he sent her to bed like a child. Now she had to do something to fix the situation.

She gasped for breath until an idea came to her. It was risky, but if it paid off, she'd be free and clear, and it would help Papa. The problem was time, and whether Molly was gullible enough to follow the plan.

She had to find a way to get the bitch alone.

***

The time flew by as Molly worked beside Tad.

"Closing time." Blue stuck his head in the kitchen door.

"I have a bit more work to do," Tad said.

"Be sure you keep the doors locked. Stay safe."

"Yes, Blue."

Molly walked to the bus stop with Blue. She shivered in the twilight.

"You've been through some traumatic experiences, maybe we should find you some counselling."

"They have something through TRU, but I might traumatize whoever I get assigned to."

"I was thinking of going through Victim Services, they might know someone who can handle what happened."

The bus pulled up and they clambered on.

The trip home was uneventful, and Molly had relaxed by the time she walked into the apartment. She still hadn't moved Harley's bed, but the sadness ached more than stabbed now.

She checked her computer for messages from Ciara and saw she had a message request.

When she clicked on it, she saw a photo of a man on the floor of some dimly lit place. What looked like blood pooled around him.

[We have ur boyfriend]

"Blue!" Molly shouted before she read the part about not telling anyone.

[Come 2 back door of Café. Bring ur key]

"What's up?"

"Does that look like Tad?" She pointed at the screen.

"Hard to say, it could be anyone." He downloaded the picture and tried a reverse search on it. "Look, it comes up as a stock photo. They want you to come to the Café alone or they'll finish him off."

"I'm calling Sergeant Ferguson."

"Good plan."

Molly dialled the non-emergency number and asked for Sergeant Ferguson.

"Sorry, Sergeant Ferguson has gone off shift. Is there someone else who can help you?"

"Is Sergeant Hassim still there?"

"Hold, please." Molly paced around holding Blue's phone until a woman's voice came on.

"Hassim here."

"Molly Callister. I got a message threatening a friend of mine."

"Describe it."

Molly read the message and described the photo.

"Stay where you are. Do not go anywhere near the Café. I'll call Ferguson, and we'll respond."

***

Ferguson really didn't like being called in, but when Hassim explained, he started snapping orders.

"Wear your vest under your winter coat. Make sure you have access to your gun."

"This isn't my first rodeo." Hassim glanced at him. "A bit nervous, are you?"

"The bad feeling is getting worse." Ferguson rubbed his temples.

"Just what we need."

"Call for backup. Ask them to hold back. We don't want to spook whoever's in there."

"Aye, aye."

They got into Ferguson's unmarked car and cruised over to the apartment where Blue gave them the keys for the front and back doors. Then they headed to the Café, passing the front first.

"No sign of anybody there," Hassim said. Ferguson's fingers drummed the steering wheel.

He drove around the back but parked out of sight of the door.

They climbed out of the car and walked along the wall. The lock on the back door had scratches on it.

"Someone's been practicing their lock picking," Ferguson said.

"Should we try spooking them?" Hassim pulled out her cell phone. "Back up on standby."

"Got it. We'll wait for your word," the response came.

"We go in quiet." Ferguson pulled out the key.

"Not a good idea if they really do have a hostage."

"Worse to go in hard." He fit the key in the lock and tried to turn it. "Must be jammed." He twisted harder.

"Wait." Hassim put a hand on his shoulder. "Something stinks."

"You're right." Ferguson pulled the key out and put his nose to the crack in the door. "Coming from inside."

"Look, they use gas." Hassim pointed at the meter.

"Bet you there's a match on the inside of the door."

"God, I hope there's no one inside." Hassim called off the backup, then contacted the fire department and explained the situation. "We'll meet you out front."

"Stay back from the doors. We're on our way."

They arrived out front, sirens blaring.

"There might be someone inside," Ferguson told them.

The bomb disposal unit showed up and wouldn't let anyone near the building until they'd cleared it. One cut a hole in the window and inserted a camera. "Looks clean. Can't see anything on the door, but there is what looks like a body by the back door." They cut a larger hole and sent in a small remote-control camera on wheels. One drove it through the Café until she spotted a match on the backdoor. "There's your booby trap. Simple but effective."

"Whoever's messed with the lock must have damaged it," Hassim said. "Thank goodness for amateurs."

"You're clear to go in."

"You're sure there's nothing on the front door?" one of the firefighters asked."

"Ninety-nine percent sure." The bomb specialist looked annoyed.

"We'll go in through the window since it's wrecked anyway." The fire chief said.

Ferguson winced as the glass shattered and two firefighters clambered carefully into the Café.

"Hey, there's someone in here," one of the firefighters yelled. Two more firefighters climbed into the Café with a stretcher.

"He's alive, but he'll have a helluva headache. Get him on oxygen." The firefighters carried him out on a stretcher.

"Gas is off, building's clear," another reported. One of the bomb squad entered wearing a mask and oxygen and walked through to disable the trap.

"You recognize the guy?" The fire chief came over to Ferguson.

"Nope, but I've never met Callister's boyfriend."

"Has a lump on his head. Says the door was open. Somebody whacked him on the head." The paramedic finished his assessment. "We'll need to get him to RIH immediately." They lifted him into the ambulance and drove off.

"If nobody's here, then where are they?" Hassim asked.

***

Blue tapped his fingers on his knees.

"I'm going to take the garbage to the chute, it's beginning to stink." Molly stood up.

"That's what you get for cooking fish for dinner." Blue tried a smile.

"It isn't the fish; probably the sour milk you threw out.

"You should stay in the apartment." Blue's smile vanished

"The chute is just down the hall; you can watch me all the way there and back."

"Fine, one step past the chute and I call the police."

"They're all at the Café, so is whoever sent that message. I'll be safe enough. I'm going nuts here, at least let me walk down the hall." Molly whined. She went to the kitchen and bagged up the garbage.

Blue walked with her to the door and watched as she walked to the end of the hall. His phone rang and he ducked in to pick it up.

When he carried it back to the door, Molly had vanished.

# Chapter 21

As soon as the cold steel pricked her neck, Molly cursed herself.

"Walk." Carolyn's voice was colder than the steel. "Try anything, make a noise and you're dead."

"You aren't going to get away with this."

"Why do people always say that?" Carolyn whined. "It's stupid." She gripped Molly's hair. "Walk. Downstairs."

They descended the stairs, the knife never wavering from Molly's neck.

"Back door," Carolyn ordered, as they walked through the basement storage.

"What do you think you're going to achieve?"

"Shut up." The knife pricked deeper. "Open the door."

The cold outside air cleared Molly's head.

*If I do what she says, I'm dead.*

She relaxed and dropped to the pavement. The knife drew blood from her neck as she fell. Carolyn tripped over her. She recovered quickly, but Molly made a split-second grab for her knife hand. Carolyn rolled away and came up in a crouch.

"I heard how you used judo shit on Cam; it just made him hornier. Won't be so easy with me." She lunged with the knife and Molly barely dodged, never mind having time to attack. Carolyn chased her around, lunging and slashing too fast for Molly to do anything but dodge. "Think you're so smart, bitch, talking about being a hooker, a junkie. Posing for the guys' attention. You broke the rule; you made me break the rule."

"What rule?" Molly gasped for air; her entire right side was covered with blood.

"'Never talk about your past. Remember you're a whore, and if the boys find out there will be trouble.' That was Papa's only rule." Carolyn spoke in measured tones like she was imitating someone.

"Papa?"

"My foster father. Did you really believe that shit about my parents taking me back? They kicked me to the curb and told me never to come back. I went into foster care. There it was in my file. Prostitute, hooker, druggie. When they weren't throwing it in my face, they were climbing into my bed. I stabbed one and did time in juvie."

"I was a foster brat, too." Molly hoped to keep Carolyn talking.

"Then Papa took me in and told me the past was a closed book. I told him I'd fucking stab him if he came into my bed. You know what he did?" Carolyn didn't sound winded at all.

"He gave you a knife?" Molly guessed and looked for a way to escape.

Carolyn sneered. "Then he gave me the rule. I could stay as long as I obeyed the rule. I could do anything else I wanted. I dated, I fucked boys, but I never broke the rule until you came along with your sympathy."

Carolyn spat at her and lunged. Molly tripped as she ducked to the side and fire burned where the knife sliced across her ribs.

"Now, I'm going to make you disappear and everyone will blame you for everything." Carolyn kicked Molly, then raised the knife.

"Freeze!" Ferguson's voice boomed. Light turned everything to stark black and white. Molly scrambled back, hoping she wouldn't be shot but unwilling to stay within Carolyn's reach.

"Bitch!" Carolyn screamed and darted toward Molly.

A crack echoed off the walls, and Carolyn slumped to the ground. Molly lay back on the asphalt and concentrated on breathing.

"Ambulance is on its way." Hassim kicked the knife away from Carolyn. "Hang in there, kid."

"Don't tell Papa I was a bad girl." Tears rolled down her face.

"What is she talking about?" Ferguson asked. Hassim used a first aid kit to try and slow the bleeding, but Carolyn had gone limp.

Molly crawled over and helped herself to gauze, holding it over the cut on her neck and the one on her ribs. The sirens grew closer as Blue came around the corner.

"Hold it there," Ferguson said. "This is a crime scene. Molly's a bit cut up, but she'll make it."

Molly couldn't stand, so she sat with her hands applying pressure to her wounds.

The ambulance arrived, and they whisked Carolyn away.

The paramedic did a better job of bandaging Molly's cuts and the other nicks and scrapes. "We'll get you to the hospital where they can stitch you up properly, but the cuts are superficial, no threat to your life." They helped Molly into a stretcher, Blue climbed into the back with her, and they rolled away. No siren for her.

She ended up waiting for hours while they tried to save Carolyn, but from the exhausted and defeated look of the doctors talking to Ferguson, Molly knew the girl had decided to die.

A nurse stitched her up and told her to drink lots of fluids. "Looks like a huge amount of blood, but you lost not much more than you would by donating."

Hassim came by to take a statement. "We'll formalize it when you feel better." She gave Molly a card with information about Victim Services.

John Brown's voice came from another room followed by a wordless cry. Molly knew that pain.

"I want to go home, Blue." Molly shook with sobs.

Blue picked up Molly and carried her out of the hospital. He put her in a cab, and they rode down the hill toward home. The back alley was filled with floodlights as the Scene of Crime people did their work.

"I should have listened to you," Molly whispered. "Carolyn might still be alive." She wiped tears from her face.

"Life happened the way it happened; no *should have, could have*." Blue helped her out of the car and up to the front door. "It will only drive you into the darkness."

# Chapter 22

**Saturday, October 16**

Blue had made her drink water until she sloshed, but Molly only had to get up once in the night. She took a couple pain pills along with more water, then went back to bed.

In the morning she dragged herself from bed and took more pain pills.

"Coffee's on," Blue said from the kitchen.

"I don't know if I want to wake up or go back to bed," Molly groaned.

"Have some coffee and decide."

"Sounds like a plan." Molly sat in her pajamas and sipped at her coffee.

"I checked with Tad. He left only a half-hour after we did. He didn't see anyone around, but he went out the front door to lock up.

"I hope you didn't tell him everything that went on last night."

"Just what he needed to know. The Café is closed until the window and gas are repaired."

"I bet he was annoyed because he'd prepped all that food."

"Most of it is in the fridge and will be fine. He's planning to cook at the Loop for Election Night."

"I need to check in with Agatha. I haven't talked with her since before the debate." Molly borrowed Blue's phone.

"I'd like to speak to Agatha Howard, please."

"One moment." The irritating hold music came on and Molly tapped her toe with impatience.

"Agatha." The familiar voice came on the line.

"Molly here, how are you feeling?"

"A lot better, the pressure is down, and they've moved me from ICU to a normal room. Erica is here. She tells me you rocked the debate."

"I did my best."

"We're going to watch the debate, then later the election."

"Say hello to Erica for me."

"Already done, sweetie." Agatha hung up.

"She sounds different."

"A whack on the head can do that." Blue poured more coffee. "She's tough though. I expect she'll be fine."

"I'm going to get dressed, then we have to go out. I need a new cellphone. I can't keep borrowing yours.

Molly put on a turtleneck sweater to mostly hide the bandage on her neck. She didn't feel like explaining it to everyone she met.

They went up to Aberdeen mall and checked out prices and plans. Molly ended up staying with her same carrier and bought a not-quite cutting-edge phone. They helped her find and restore her data from the old phone, except what was encrypted, which wasn't much anyway. Immediately it started pinging and wouldn't stop.

"Somebody misses you." The girl behind the counter smirked.

"When Ciara said she was leaving messages, she wasn't kidding." The phone finally caught up with Ciara's texts, so Molly sent a message back to let Ciara know she had a phone again.

They did a bit of shopping, and Blue convinced Molly to buy some new clothes.

"Winter is coming, and you'll need to be warm."

They ate at the food court, then rode the bus home.

"Let's put this away, then go vote," Blue said. They walked to the poll and voted. A news team caught them, and Molly had to give an impromptu interview.

"Exit polls are suggesting that a lot of people would have voted for you if you'd run. Are you planning to take another run at the job?"

"I honestly don't know. I guess it depends on how well the City does with improving social services and increasing housing stock for low-income people."

"You said in your answer to the question of social workers responding to welfare checks and mental health concerns, that you'd take the job if they offered it. Are you still planning that?"

"Let's wait until they make the offer." Molly laughed. "I do have two terms of school left before I graduate."

"There was a lot of controversy around your possible involvement with the murder of Cameron Robinson. Any comment?"

"I will let the police make a statement on that when they are ready."

"What will you do if you win?"

"If Agatha wins, I will continue to support her as mayor."

"That was Molly Callister, spokesperson for the Agatha Howard campaign."

Molly made her escape as the journalists found another person to interview.

"You handled that well." Blue nudged her. "There may be a career in politics for you yet."

She leaned her head on his shoulder for a moment.

"Thanks, Blue, I am very lucky that you found me."

"I feel the same way."

***

Molly woke up to the sounds of conversation. She went out to the living room to find Hanna and Ciara drinking tea with Blue.

"Rough week." Hanna handed Molly a cup. "Drink some tea and tell us about it."

"I don't know, I think it started more than a week ago, but the last week was intense. It doesn't help that I feel like I was kicked around like a soccer ball."

"At least you have cool new scars to show you survived," Ciara said.

"Ciara!" Hanna glowered at the girl.

"I don't know about the cool bit, but I did indeed survive." Molly sipped the tea. "One of your special blends."

"I helped pick the leaves." Ciara grinned. "Grandma showed me all kinds of neat stuff."

"Good for you." Molly sighed. "I'd love to go out with you sometime."

"Anytime. I'll call you up the next time I'm going out." Hanna smiled at Molly.

"I drink so much of the tea; I should know where it comes from."

"Always a good idea." Hanna nodded.

"So we're going to the party," Ciara said. "You should dress up nicer; you're going to be on tv."

"Maybe you could help me choose an outfit." Molly looked at the clock. "We'll do that, then have supper before we go."

Molly asked, "So how are you getting along with your grandma?" Ciara pulled out clothes and put them on the bed

"Better, I guess. She still expects me to know what to do."

"When you were gathering medicine, did she tell you what to do?"

"No, she just told me to watch, then let me try."

"Maybe watch your grandma, then try to act the way that feels right. You need to find your own way but also learn from people who've made mistakes, so you don't need to."

"I guess. It sounds like a lot of work."

"Is it any more work than fighting all the time?"

"Maybe." Ciara handed Molly a turtleneck shirt. "Wear this instead of that bulky thing, then you can put a jacket over it. Don't you own any skirts?"

"I'm not much for skirts."

"Even I know you can't dress up without a skirt. I'll make you a ribbon skirt for next time." Ciara twirled, showing off her outfit.

"Next time?" Molly raised an eyebrow.

"There are always times to dress up."

"You are right about that." Molly laughed.

Molly and Hanna cooked supper, talking about food and inconsequentials. Hanna drove them to the Loop.

There were already a lot of people there. Agatha and Erica had joined by Facebook messenger.

"Hi, good to see you in person," Molly said. "So to speak."

"Erica has been telling me how hard you worked getting ready for the debate. Your name really should be the one on the ballot."

"Don't think I'm ready for that." Molly held up a hand. "I need to finish my degree."

"Next election is four years away." Agatha laughed. "Plenty of time to change your mind."

The numbers trickled in from the polls. As Molly expected, they were nowhere near the front runners, but she and Paul Admanson were running neck and neck.

The party atmosphere continued until the results were declared. Molly called the new mayor to congratulate her and wish her well.

"You ran quite the campaign, Molly, you and Agatha both." They went back to their supporters.

"So?" Ciara asked.

"She congratulated us on running a good campaign."

Molly talked to Agatha before the older woman went to sleep.

"It is a privilege to have worked for you.   I learned a huge amount."

"Next time you run, and I'll be your manager." Agatha laughed.

"Congratulations, Molly." Tad took her hand and squeezed it. "Agatha's name was on the ballot, but I voted for you."

***

## Monday, October 18

Monday at university was subdued after Cameron and Carolyn's deaths, and she went through her classes on autopilot. Her professors found a way to bring the election into their lectures and asked Molly for her input, then challenged the class.

"Community social work, in particular, has always had a strong political side." Professor Czysiki said. "Advocacy means being aware of where the power is and working to correct the imbalance. We don't want to just help people survive but make the system into one where survival isn't a daily battle."

# Chapter 23
**Tuesday, October 18**

Molly was more nervous about her date with Tad than she'd been for the All-Candidates Meeting. She called in Ciara for help.

"What am I supposed to do?" Molly flopped back on the bed, covered with rejected outfits.

"Be yourself."

"I've never been on a date before. What will he expect?"

"If he's smart, he won't expect anything but having a nice night out." Ciara sounded like she was quoting her grandma.

"Have you been on a date?"

"Nah, Grandma says to wait. Be friends with the boys, but not to let them, or the girls, push me into anything I'm not ready for."

"Do you listen to her?"

"Mostly." Ciara grinned.

They decided on an outfit, and Molly waited for Tad to arrive.

He buzzed at the door, and she let him in.

"You look nice." He handed her some flowers and Molly tried to remember if she'd ever got flowers before. She found a jug to put them in.

"Thank you, they are beautiful."

"We'd better go to get a good seat," Tad said. "I borrowed my dad's car; I didn't think you'd want to ride the bus."

"Let's go then." Molly followed him out the door.

The drive to the Paramount was silent. Not like when she and Blue sat without talking, more like neither of them knew how to break the silence. Molly ran her hand over the leather upholstery and wished they'd taken the bus; she was comfortable in buses.

In the theatre, there was only a spattering of people.

"You choose a seat," Molly said. "I haven't been to a movie in ages."

They settled in, then Tad sat up. "I forgot popcorn."

Molly grabbed his hand. "That's okay, I'm not sure I could eat it."

Tad settled back but didn't let go of her hand. Molly didn't mind; it settled the butterflies in her stomach.

The movie came on and as it progressed, Tad fidgeted more.

"Relax," Molly whispered. "It isn't your fault it is the worst movie ever made."

"It is bad, but I don't know if it compares with *Plan 9 from Outer Space.*"

"I've never heard of it."

"It's an old black and white movie which is so bad it is hilariously funny."

"Sounds like fun. We'll have to watch it someday."

When the movie ended, they went to the Tim Hortons on Eighth and laughed about the film.

"I kept waiting for a plot to jump out and scare us," Molly said.

"Who knew it would develop a plot in the last minutes of the movie."

Tad drove them back to the apartment, then walked her to the door.

"May I kiss you goodnight?" Tad asked and Molly stiffened.

"I don't think I'm ready for that."

"Okay." Tad hugged her.

"Thanks for treating me like a normal girl."

"Why would I treat you any differently?"

"You know, because of who I was."

"Brave, resourceful, kind?" Tad stepped back. "We all have our stories, Molly."

"I'd like to hear more of yours."

"Then you'll go out with me again?" Tad's eyes lit up.

"Next time, I choose the movie."

# Other books by Alex
## Series:

### Calliope Books
Calliope and the Sea Serpent
Calliope and the Royal Engineers
The Third Prince and the Enemy's Daughter
Calliope and the Kershan Empire

### Spruce Bay Books
Wendigo Whispers
Cry of the White Moose
Disputed Rock

### The Belandria Tarot
The Devil Reversed
The Regent's Reign
The Empire Unbalanced
The World Widens
The Fury Unleashed

### Blue in Kamloops
Tranquille Dark
Columbia Smoke

Victoria Run

**The Call**
Call of a Hero

# Stand-alone books:

Leedles and the Golden Tree
Generation Gap
The Gods Above
Tales of Light and Dark
Like Mushrooms (poetry and photography)
The Heronmaster
Blood and Sparkles, and other stories
Princess of Boring
By the Book
Sarcasm is My Superpower
Playing on Yggdrasil
The Unenchanted Princess

Read short stories and excerpts from his novels
at alexmcgilvery.com